Belle Otis

The Diary of a Milliner

Belle Otis

The Diary of a Milliner

ISBN/EAN: 9783743372986

Manufactured in Europe, USA, Canada, Australia, Japa

Cover: Foto ©Andreas Hilbeck / pixelio.de

Manufactured and distributed by brebook publishing software (www.brebook.com)

Belle Otis

The Diary of a Milliner

THE

DIARY OF A MILLINER.

BY

BELLE OTIS.

NEW YORK:
PUBLISHED BY HURD AND HOUGHTON,
459 BROOME STREET.
1867.

RIVERSIDE, CAMBRIDGE:
STEREOTYPED AND PRINTED BY
H. O. HOUGHTON AND COMPANY.

PREFACE.

WHEN I went into business I had very correct ideas of integrity in the abstract, and they were methodically embodied in the theory which I laid out for practice. If they have become modified in the use, it is the result of knowledge acquired by experience.

I intended to make steady, reasonable profits. I had no idea of the fluctuation in prices which might interfere with my purpose. I intended to represent my goods just as they were, and, by that practice, to obtain a reputation for reliability that would command the respect and patronage — patronage certainly, that was the essential point to be gained — of a reasonable class of people.

My theory was a good one. If it was imperfect, charity suggests that, it was like all theories formed without practical knowledge of the subject treated. Ignorance of my own, and the human nature of others under the peculiar conditions of trader and customer, helped to make the theory. Experience very soon remedied that disadvantage.

I tried to manage well the various kinds of human nature with which I came in contact. At least, so to manage them as to enable me to earn the means to pay my honest debts for food and clothing.

How reasonable I have found reasonable people when their purses were the medium of intercourse, my Journal will relate. How reliable I have been able to prove myself, in order to meet the various exigencies presented to my management by the various characters with whom I have dealt, the same Journal will set forth.

It is well to premise that the differences of opinion upon special cases of integrity are as various and numerous as the individual interests that judge them. And because individual instances are so numerous, investigation must be confined to a limited number of circumstances. To become acquainted with every business transaction which has ever taken place between man and man, or woman and woman, and determine its moral merits, would require more time and wisdom than one person can conveniently command.

I do not relate what I have learned about myself and others, through the education of business transactions, supposing that I can work reformation in one or the other party.

I made my notes and observations for my own entertainment: I give them to the public for the same reason, or for any other which my readers may see fit to ascribe to me.

If I have n't extenuated the faults of my customers, I have " set down naught in malice " against them. I can say, almost unexceptionally of them, " With all thy faults I love thee still." I am not a solitary tradeswoman in saying that; most others can, with all truthfulness, enunciate the same sentiment, so far as the society of their customers is given them for purposes of trade.

I did not intend to state, although a class of minds might infer that I insinuated such a fact, that I feel toward every one of my customers the love of complacency, that would desire to associate with them because they are personally agreeable to me.

You see, by this example, how easy it is to give our own coloring to the statements of others, draw wrong inferences, and come to irrelevant conclusions from forced premises. But there is a liking necessarily engendered when association brings financial benefit to one or both parties associating together. Therefore, Mr. Observer, when you see a merchant pat his customer on the shoulder, plaster him all over with compliments, and wind up with the irresistible argument, " I sell this kind of goods so-and-so to my other customers, but as it is *you*, I 'll call it twenty per cent. less," — don't mark that man down a liar and hypocrite, fawning on his victim to lure his money from him in a good bargain. He really feels complacently and kindly. He may not analyze his state of mind to understand the cause that produced it; but he wishes his customer to be in receipt of the state of his affections. If his manner develop an unnecessary excess of attachment to accomplish the purpose in view, it is because he is constitutionally demonstrative, and extremely susceptible to favors conferred. He may indulge his natural demonstrativeness and susceptibility to a fault. He may cultivate the traits till they are ludicrously apparent to his customers, and become a topic of discussion and merriment among them. Still, the vanity of the said customers, not the flattering behavior of the merchant, imposes upon the understanding, and leads captive the credulity of the sophisticated buyer. And in contravention of his assertion that such stuff has no influence upon his strong common sense, he goes again and again to purchase where he gets goods twenty per cent. less than other customers, and affectionate treatment thrown in. There is evidently love on both sides, however each party, when separate, may represent the matter.

Without apology I open the pages of my Diary, and give you my observations on my customers and myself; not in the shadow of forthcoming events, or in the retrospective reflection of the past, but in the unmistakable light of present transactions.

I do not send them forth bearing the unctuous invocation that they may be blest to the good of some offending sinner; but I may be allowed to indulge the wish, not accompanied by the slightest expectation, that they may be set home to some woman's heart, receive sufficient attention to become digested by her good sense, and lead her to think on her ways during the performance of her practical duties in shopping.

When one submits himself to reflection on any subject connected with his personal habits, self-education has commenced, and the most difficult step is taken. The satisfaction with one's own sayings and

doings which excludes self-examination, is the greatest obstacle to a change of views and manners,
where such a change may seem desirable to the
view of friends and acquaintances. And the desir-
ableness of such changes is usually far more obvi-
ous to observers than to those directly and actively
engaged in the practice of the habits under consideration.

DIARY OF A MILLINER.

I.

I AM left a widow with the necessity upon me of getting my own living, and an abundance of vitality and energy wherewith to accomplish it. There is a something telling me it is for my good to be doing something. Doing! that is the word, — let the action be suited to it.

But to do something which earns a living will mark me masculine and vulgar. I can live with my relatives, and retain my standing in society. Eat the bread of dependence? No! no! The bread of honest industry, or vulgarity, is preferable. But the world! but society! Bah! what is society? I am society. If I can't make myself the best of society for myself I shall be of all women most miserable.

I am told that it is not genteel and fashionable for young ladies to work. It is an enigma to me why it is genteel for a mother to work, and vulgar for a daughter to do so. If the daughter lose caste by being industrious, why not the mother! I am referred to fashion to solve it. I have never yet

1

been able to pin that omnipresent, intangible poten-
tate down to explain any ukase that is issued in her
name.   In consequence, refusing to submit to her
administration, I become a law unto myself.

I decide on going to work because it suits my
pleasure so to do.   What shall I undertake?   Shall
I go on a salary, or engage in some business of my
own?   Why should I go on a salary when I am as
capable of managing a business, and obtaining all the
profits of it as the one who might employ me.   But
what business can a woman establish herself in?
men monopolize every thing.

I begin to see some point to the woman's rights
question.   Why is there a masculine monopoly of
business?   Why shouldn't woman compete with man
in the race for earning money and getting a living?
There are certainly no legal objections to her doing
it; no moral ones that I can see.   The chief difficulty appears to lie in her own capacity, or rather
lack of capacity, physical and mental, and in the
social atmosphere with which she is surrounded.

To be sure woman in her present *status* is not
fitted to undertake all kinds of business.   Her manner of dress, and other habits, would make it rather
inconvenient for her to go to the mast-head in a gale,
or handle goods in a wholesale grocery establishment.   She has as much as she can attend to out-
of-doors to hold up her trailing garments, adjust her
sun-shade, and make a graceful appearance in the
eyes of the other sex.

I can't change the social condition of woman. My wisdom is to make the best of it. There must be some kinds of business that a woman can undertake.

On thinking it over nothing presents itself but a fancy-goods store, dress-making, millinery, or a candy shop. There are but few kinds to choose from, but business will be independence. There will be no one to say me aye or nay, and that will be a glorious state of existence, even if I flourish in a candy shop.

I did love you dearly, Will; but I will own to one decided objection to married life. I was often obliged to go one way when I wished to go another. Every woman must do that sometimes if she have ever so loving a lord. Perhaps I am a little premature in exulting over independence in a candy shop. The fact presents itself to my attention that the circumstances of buying and selling candy may intervene between me and independence. The thought suggests itself that the circumstances attending such employment may control me with quite as irksome an authority as the commands of married rule.

I wonder if there is any position of entire independence in life. I can think of none but that of a hermit in a cave, and he can't be independent of heat and cold, hunger and thirst, and the provision to be made for those exigencies. I might as well rest contented on that point. There is no such

thing as independence without some qualification.
I might as well accept the position of servitude to
circumstances which must issue in servitude to people, and then how fares independence ? Its existence
is among the myths.

Looking it over in all its bearings, as any prudent
woman would do, I think millinery will suit me
better than either of the other branches of trade
under consideration, and millinery it shall be. I
must go into a store to learn some of the intricacies
of trade before I run any risks. I must get some
practical knowledge of those perplexing phrases,
percentage, profits, losses, &c. To me they are sci-
entific technicalities.

APRIL 2, 18—,

I could cry, Eureka ! I have found, not my paradise exactly, but the way to it. I have found the
first stepping-stone to wealth, and I would say independence, only that I am a little shy of that long
word. Not because I am timid, no, no ! I have
never yet been convicted of indulging in that sin ;
but when I have floundered in deep water once,
and failed to find a bottom, I am a little cautious
about venturing in again. That is what is called
learning wisdom by experience, I think.

I have found a chance to learn to do business in
one of the largest millinery establishments on Wash-
ington Street, and I have already earned money
enough, in imagination, to immortalize my name
through thousands of succeeding generations. How ?

By establishing Homes for elderly ladies, Foundling Asylums, Wanderers' Retreats, and every thing else that will beautify and make a paradise of this suffering world.

Plodding women may sit down to the restraints of married life in order to obtain the remuneration of a living, and a poor one at that, without the power of making it better; but as for me, instead of marrying again I choose business. I would like the opportunity of spreading my individual self before the world in manly — womanly independence. How naturally that word comes up at every turn to bother one. A woman may — a man must — what? Spread himself, earn money, and rear monuments to commend himself to posterity? He must go out into the world and earn a living by hard knocks, or soft knocks just as his lot is cast. That is his freedom, his independence, and circumstances fetter him to it, — the circumstance of choice between that and starvation. A hard lot it sometimes seems, but man's occupation in life is to get a living; without the stimulus of that necessity what does he become? Look at the heirs of wealth for an answer. His pride to get a good living, a respectable or luxurious living keeps his industry in exercise. His ambition, which sealed his fall, stirs him to attain godlike heights among the fallen. Pride, his destroyer, becomes his savior.

Man's attributes are arranged on a pivot to turn to good or evil as he wills. Or, if he has no moral ballast, to turn as circumstances shape them. There is very little difference between us as I am situated. I feel myself in manly circumstances in the regard of getting a living. I can also boast myself in his independence. I am at liberty to make my choice of an occupation. I shall be independent in spending my earnings as I like. Not precisely? I am in the leashes there. I am hand-cuffed by the necessity of paying for my food, clothing, and shelter. There is no such thing as independence. Yes, I am independent to go about the employment which I have chosen. That is, if no sickness, or accident, or other untoward circumstance intervenes.

APRIL 3, 18—.

I have been where business was transacted to-day. It seems strange to be standing behind a counter, showing people goods, recommending them, and telling prices. Recommending them, — that is the secret of selling, and to sell is the sole motive of standing behind a counter. I begin to see into it. The character is to be understood, and the particular motive that will induce to buy is to be placed before a customer. Some expose themselves in every sentence they utter; but not every one. My art is to fathom the motive, and suit it. The human face divine is an excellent index. I find that I can tell by a glance whether the article sought for suits by the expression of the face. We hear telltale countenances spoken of as something out of the common way; but I never saw a face on which a tale was not written, and being constantly continued in one life-long serial.

APRIL 4, 18—.

I am getting on bravely with trade as an art. I have got my bearings, and am ready to take observations.

Out of the vast swarms of butterflies that have lighted in our store to-day to gather ribbons and flowers there were scarcely any but anxious faces. The perplexity of choosing adornments added little to their charms. Strange how the workings of the inner, stamp themselves on the lineaments of the outer man, or woman. Strange, incomprehensible phenomenon is the human dual!

As I step from one sphere of employment to another, it is like going from one nation to another, people exhibit themselves in different spheres so differently. Is it deceit that makes a woman appear to-day noble, generous, disinterested, and to-morrow mean, miserly, hard? No! she acts herself in both instances. To-day she is surrounded by circumstances that draw out all that is noble and generous in her character. To-morrow circumstances throw her into the mire of worldliness; cupidity rules, and drags her into meanness and hard-faced chaffering for lucre. God's grace, if always in exercise, would render her always the nobly good; but alas! somebody that dwells at the opposite side of creation from the Holy Father gets possession of the inner temple, and behold he possesses the whole

structure with his greedy designs. He seals the
heart with his seal, and stamps the face with his
demoniac stamp. Self-ignorance, and self-righte-
ousness complete his work.

But many are deceitful and try to appear to others
what they are not! Certainly, in conventional intercourse where every one is a sham; but in shopping a woman forgets to hold up her mantle of deceit ; it falls, and behold a naked human heart!

To appear good is the effort of all. To be good in
order to appear so is the effort of a few. Over those
who try to rule their evil dispositions, and stimulate
their good ones to growth in contravention of circumstances, circumstances lose much of their control.
Through God's grace alone, in constant exercise,
can the demon in the human heart be made to grow
small, and the angel to grow large. Shopping af-
fords an illimitable atmosphere in which to exercise
the angel, or the demon. It is a mixed, muddy,
confused atmosphere, and the two spirits are very
apt to get confounded ; and in consequence the one
gets the exercise which was intended for the other.
The one being arrogant in its habits, and the other
retiring, — the angel needs encouragement and assistance, even force, to get it into the atmosphere
of active life, while the other rushes forward in hot
haste to its social revelries.

Well, as the ladies' faces changed from one perplexity to another, each changing emotion adding its
own peculiar disembellishment, an ill-natured sug-

gestion, which I long ago heard about the beauty
of the fair tenants of the " Hub " recurred to me,
and I thought the originator of it must have been
a milliner, or some other trades-person. Viewed in
the light of trade — I say it to you my Diary in
confidence — their reputation for plainness is based
upon a foundation which will last through all time,
and remain impregnable to all assaults, — *i. e.* the
truth.

Some countenances became thoroughly repulsive
under the influence of contending emotions, — anxiety to obtain something to modify natural asperities,
and fear of parting with the money to pay for it.

The prominent feature in to-day's trade has been
the surprise expressed at the rise in prices. The war
has raised the price of bonnets as well as of every
thing else, and it is like a drama to witness the contortions, and hear the exclamations of a novice in
he present era of shopping.

" Oh my soul ! what a price ! " with elevated eye-
brows, and uplifted hands iterated and reiterated·a
lady to whom I had told the cost of a bonnet which
she was examining with a view to purchase. Her
overflowing astonishment continued, for some five
minutes, to find vent in repeating that one elegant
exclamation, " Oh my soul ! what a price ! "

There is nothing like giving a lady time to collect
herself when agitated by an unexpected event; or
rather to let off in her own way the mental gas
which surprise or vexation, or both combined, is sure

to generate in her gentle imagination. While she occupied herself in that involuntary employment I very leisurely set myself to observe her manners, and analyze her expression.

I was a little puzzled to understand why she should call upon her soul in this surprising dilemma. If she had apostrophized her expensive head, instead of the spiritual element of her constituency, I could have readily understood the connection between the object of her indignation and the expression of it. But the immortal, just at that moment, was the element of her duality which had the least interest in her employment. Not one penny was in consideration for its adorning, however important she might consider attention to its concerns in the abstract to be.

As attention to the concerns of the soul are no part of the millinery business, I did n't see fit to remind her of the misnomer which she had committed. Such a digression might have interfered with my opportunity of selling her a bonnet, or to a rapid consummation of that prospective event; so I quietly remarked, —

" We consider that a very reasonable price for the times."

" Reasonable ! " she echoed; "was there ever any reason in the price of a milliner ? "

I saw then, distinctly, that her indignation was directed, not towards the soul she had adjured, or the offending head which had suggested itself to my thoughts as a very proper object of wrath, in view of its misdemeanors in making trouble and expense; but toward the offending craft to which I had attached myself with such brilliant expectations.

My will was roused by what I considered the uncalled-for explosion. I, at least, was no culprit, and deserved no such accusations. I decided in my own mind that she would in all probability buy that bonnet, and pay the price I asked her. My wisdom was to conceal the conclusion I had reached, and also the line of policy I had decided to pursue in order to accomplish my object. Was I deceitful? No! only exercising proper caution. Mine was a cool, calculating retaliation, far more culpable than the hasty anger that excited it, — perhaps. At first I wished to sell the bonnet; her last expression determined me to do it.

I wonder if the inner emotions, which I then entertained, were the workings of the inner life of which poets sing. If so, the inner singing may become any thing but musical. Mine was any thing but music at that moment, but I spoke blandly.

" The bonnet is well suited to your complexion and figure," was the exordium to my design. I saw that it took. The exordium, or the bonnet, I did n't know which, nor did it matter so long as her fancy was captivated. I went on to arrange my peroration as skillfully as possible to consummate my sale. I must arouse no opposition by contradicting her established idea of high prices, but conciliate by falling in with it, so I said, in a sympathetic tone, " You are correct. The price is high compared with what it would have been a year ago." Now her fears must be aroused, and worked upon, of suffering still more in her purse by delay to purchase. I added, " But not so high as it will inevitably be in a few days. Prices have gone up surprisingly within the last twenty-four hours."

" So I 've heard," she replied, "and I 've come out to see what I can do for myself."

I saw I had my finger on the right key, and I pressed a little harder. " Government expenses must increase — taxes must be heavier in order to pay them — goods must necessarily be higher — it is wisdom to buy now if you can find what is suited to you, and that bonnet is just the thing !"

" So my husband says, — he is in business," she replied thoughtfully. I saw that I nearly had her, so I continued to enlarge upon the basis of her fears, till I really made the poor little financier think if she waited another day, or even took time to " look," prices would outstrip her in travelling upward, and she would be obliged to pay much more than I asked her for that bonnet, for a poorer one. I begin to see into the art of getting up a panic.

" I like the bonnet — but, oh my soul ! what a price ! "

" It is a great price," I replied slowly ; " but it may be greater." I was willing to give line upon line and precept upon precept, both here and there in abundance, in order to accomplish my object. I went over the whole ground of the probable, inevitable rise of goods again with admirable patience, — admirable to myself, — there was no one else to admire.

While I was admiring myself, and talking to her, I was still accomplishing a process of observation upon what I heard, and was engaged in. Life is twofold, dual, the Swedenborgians have it. I have established it to be three.

The lady I was selling the bonnet to was living the twofold life. The inner lay within the purse, and the outer consisted of calculations to adorn the outer woman — man and woman being in the generic sense considered one person in this connection. Such a platitude can hardly be called a candid propounding of the Swedenborgian doctrine of dual life.

I shall be unable to class my threefold existence, which I am confident was in operation at the time, in any system of theology with which I am acquainted. It may possibly come under some head of metaphysics ; but what head I have n't time just now to examine.

While I was enlarging upon the profitable operation of purchasing immediately, profitable to her if she bought the bonnet, I could hardly be supposed, under the circumstances, to be managing for any one else. Wonderful disinterestedness ! how the newspapers would magnify such an item if they got hold of it. I was getting up a little episode within my third self by way of retaliation for the thrust she gave my' chosen craft at the commencement of her trade.

It was a spiteful little episode, but it proved a wonderful counter irritant in relieving the words I saw fit to utter pleasantly. It was got up in this wise. It is our business; and your object, just now, to attend to the adorning of your earthly tabernacle. As for the tricking out of your immortal soul, it will take something more than flowers and laces and ribbons to make it presentable in the society of those who will be judges of its beauty.

When you reach those altitudes I may be called upon to give attention to very important business of my own so that I cannot notice you at all; but I feel it to be my privilege, just now, to exercise all the functions of the inner life toward you.

Patience and persistence prevailed. I sold her the bonnet.

II.

THE book, in the Book of books, which recommends itself to a person in trade on account of its. peculiar adaptation to his moral necessities, as an example and teacher, is the one which recounts the crosses, and the fortitude with which they were borne, of that inimitable patriarch whose given and family name are comprised in that of Job.

The name indicates to every hearer, when used, that moral quality denominated patience. In order to set forth the character, and distinguish from other virtues or religious attainments the extent of it desirable to be obtained in order to sustain the trader under his annoyances, an infant designed for business employment might as well be presented at the font under the compound name of Job Job. The significance of such an act to point at the truth that a double portion of the saintly virtue which distinguished his renowned and immortal prototype is invited, through the sacrament celebrated, to permeate his moral constitution in infancy, so that it may grow with his growth and strengthen with his strength. The utility of such a proceeding would scarcely be questioned by the said trader presump-

tive when he has arrived at manhood, and entered
upon his labors, *i. e.*, if he intends to trade honestly.

After the trader presumptive is old enough, he
might with profit be sent to school where a session
was held every day to investigate the moral construction of the aforesaid patriarch's character.   In order
to obtain the full benefit of such an arrangement,
this exercise ought to be continued, without the interruption of holidays, so that the stream of fitting
instruction for after life may remain unbroken.

It would be indispensable to continue the exercise
after he has entered a store preparatory to commencing business for himself.

If he is so opinionated (young people are apt to
indulge a great opinion of their own abilities, owing
to their lack of self-knowledge) as to think himself
too much of a man to require the assistance of such
childish instruction, he will soon change his mind,
learn wisdom by the things from which he suffers,
and go back to it as the salt of his life, the only
preservation of his success.

To illustrate the importance of what I have been
saying I will tell a tale of to-day.   Those who like
to turn every thing to instruction may whittle a moral
therefrom.

A well-dressed lady came up to me, and asked me
to show her some of our handsomest bonnets.

I asked. "Are you looking for any particular style
or color?"

"No.   I wish to see what will become me best."

She deliberately took off her own bonnet and commenced trying those that were on the saloon table. One after one she took them up, and put them on her head, till she had seen about thirty casting their differently combined tints over her complexion. She invited my comments and suggestions upon each one. She viewed herself in each in the five mirrors of the saloon, in all the various lights she could command, and placed herself in every conceivable attitude before them.

One thing or another was at fault in every one of them. She had asked the price of all, and cheapened each to the lowest possible fraction for which they could be bought.

She then went to the side-table, and performed the same operation upon herself with fifteen or twenty more. There were none that exactly suited.

"Have n't you some put away in drawers?" she asked. I went the same rounds with a dozen drawers containing six or eight bonnets apiece.

When those were exhausted she pointed to the window, and asked if I would be kind enough to bring her two handsome bonnets that were hanging there.

Something in the inner life, probably it was that attribute of the dual denominated penetration, admonished me that she did n't wish to purchase a bonnet, but was seeking an afternoon's entertainment at our expense. Another something, whether it was a spirit tapping, tapping at the inner door

2

I know not, admonished me that there are times when to practice the forbearing policy of the remarkable patriarch, of whom I have been speaking, is to cast pearls before swine. Instead of starting for the desired bonnets, I looked her steadily in the eye while I modulated my voice to a very respectful tone, and replied : —

"If you really wish to buy a bonnet, I will go down and get them; but I fear they will suit you no better than the others have done."

She saw that her *rolé* was played to the end, and a successful actress she had proved herself. She had confined her audience in the closest attention for about two hours. The other two bonnets were beyond her reach. With the most inimitable coolness and unconcern she looked me back and replied : —

"I don't wish to buy a bonnet. I bought mine last week."

If she had struck me in the face I would n't have been more startled and surprised than I was at the exhibition of such boldness. I could scarce refrain from crying out, " O shame, where hides thy blush ! "

After a moment, the ease with which she had accomplished her consummate piece of impudence moderated my indignation to a sort of admiration. I would like to know more about you, I thought.

I could conceive of no motive that could induce a lady — so she appeared on the surface — to make so irredeemably mean an exhibition of herself. I abnegated self in apparent interest in her affairs, and quietly asked : —

" If you did n't wish to purchase, why have you tried so many bonnets ? "

" I wanted to find out your prices, to see if I had got cheated in mine. If I did I 'll never trade at the place where I bought it again."

She had told me the truth, but not the whole truth. I like to sift truth to the bottom, so I pursued : —

" You need n't have tried all those bonnets to have found out the prices. I would have told you that, with pleasure, if it would have given you satisfaction."

" Oh, I wanted to see, too, if you had a bonnet in your store more becoming to me than mine. My milliner told me if I could find one in the whole city more so I might keep the bonnet and she would give me the money back ! "

Shades of meanness ! shrieked the inner, have you unlocked your gates to punish my ignorance of what lies within a human heart? Ignorance is bliss ! — wisdom is folly ! — is misery ! Have I part and lot in this matter of humanity? Let me hide my head in the sands of ignorance, and believe myself unseen if I must present such a spectacle to those who are looking at me ! That was doubtless the condition of my customer. Her eyes only were covered, but the great misshapen body of her moral deformity was looming up before my sight.

" Would you take the money if you could find
the bonnet ? " I asked in perfect composure.

" Yes, I would take the money and leave the bonnet, to punish her for talking so. She deserves it."
What an immense beam sported before that woman's sight.

I had nothing to say to such a proceeding, but I
presume she noticed the look of surprise that passed
over my countenance, and she continued : " I have n't
worn it but three times, — once to church, once out
to Roxbury, and once to the Museum."

My disgust had grown too deep for utterance by
word or look. I stood " stock still."

She must have supposed me perplexed, or not
quite satisfied, and she went on to explain her motives further. " Store-keepers do tell such shocking
lies in order to sell their goods, I see no other way
but to keep strict watch of them, and bring them up
to the mark when they overreach and don't tell
the truth."

I begin to understand the cause of the antagonism
which is instituted between customers and traders.
The sin of the individual is visited upon the craft.
The object of one is to buy and sell and get gain
at all events. The old Quaker's advice to his son
being put in practice, — " Get money honestly if thee
can, my boy, but don't fail to get it." All are judged
by what one does ; and, sooth to say, those who employ their time in tracking culprits might be profit-
ably employed in practicing the advice, " Physician,

heal thyself." Those that buy are equally anxious
to get gain with those that sell, — hence the con-
flict.

The inner dual had, all this time, been converting
itself into an alembic, slowly and surely, wherein to
ferment indignation and wrath. If it could have
generated tribulation and anguish for that woman
it would have rejoiced in exercising its capacity at
that time. Just at this point it arrived at culmi-
nation. A moment of silence, then the retort emitted
its contents. Not in a fiery stream of rebuke, but in
cool, sarcastic inquiry that humbly sought instruction as to the quality of morals.

" Which do you think the greater wrong, for you
to come here with a lie in all your actions — your
pretence was to buy a bonnet — make use of that
pretence to steal my time, which is the money of my
employer — I might have sold several bonnets while
I have been attending to you — or for a store-keeper
to deceive you, and take more than a reasonable
profit from you ? If you will explain the difference
the knowledge will be gratefully received."

She belonged to the class that put on the cheek
and push themselves. She was nothing daunted by
the inquiry, but with an impertinent toss of her head
replied : —

" You are here to show goods, and wait upon customers. I have been in stores before when they
were angry because I did n't buy."

" Yes, ma'am ; we are here to wait upon customers ;

but you are not a customer. Customers buy goods, and pay us for the time we spend waiting upon them in the profits we make. But you came here with no such intention."

She did n't seem disposed to pursue the discussion further; but with the most unblushing effrontery, or was it ignorance? thanked me for my politeness, bade me good afternoon, and left the store.

Is it very wonderful that store-keepers become impatient sometimes, even to rudeness?

If I had followed the bent of my inclination I should have caught her by the dress, and compelled her to remain while I extemporized a short and pungent discourse for her benefit.

My impromptu text would have been, "The heart is deceitful above all things, and desperately wicked." In my then state of mind, and earnestness to sustain the proposition, I might have exaggerated the desperate wickedness into total depravity.

My firstly would have sustained the division that the heart first tries to deceive itself; in which endeavor it usually succeeds, having but little opposition to encounter from the person attacked, and much necessary assistance given. My practical observation on that head would have been, Thou art the woman!

My secondly, that it then attempts to impose upon others; but fails frequently for the want of proper material to impose upon, and the necessary assistance required to insure success. My practical observation on that head would have been, You cannot impose upon others because they see through you, and do not choose to be imposed upon. She might have answered, I managed to do so for a short time.

I should then have closed the exercises by singing her a hymn, composed by an old and popular poet, commencing, —

> " O wad some power the giftie gie us,
> To see oursels as ithers see us,
> It would frae mony a blunder free us."

The outer life made no sign. I stood in silent composure, watched her take in her phylacteries, and sweep in studied complacency out of the store.

Instead of holding the meeting contemplated, to produce her possible conviction and conversion, the inner dual contented itself with pronouncing a benediction upon her departure after this wise, — " Sackcloth and ashes are fitting fabrics to adorn such inner temples as yours. May a tender Father pity the infinitesimality of your morals, and enlarge your borders, if there is breadth enough in His grace to add to your knowledge."

I turned and went to wait upon another lady — lady? — woman, woman? — female. That will do. Who can wonder at the scruple?

" Well," said the gentleman in whose store I was, and who had watched the whole affair, " what is your opinion now of the high and mighty power of urbanity in teaching such a woman good manners in shopping ?"

" She must be an unusual case, and unreformable by human instrumentality. Only an arrow from God's own quiver can penetrate such ossified selfishness, and reform such unmitigated low breeding. Reformation of manners must come through reformation of morals."

" I should have sent her out of the store long before she left; but I saw you were getting your learning."

" That would have been very bad manners."

" It would have been just what she deserved. The only way to teach such people any thing is to give them a sound rating. They consider stores as benevolent institutions for the benefit of the public. Our time is nothing ; the loss we sustain in the handling of our goods is what they take without the slightest consideration. A sound rating was just what she needed, and what she would have got, only I wanted to see how you would manage."

" To have lost my temper, and given her a scolding would have been to put myself on her level, instead of bringing her up to what I consider the proper way to behave. In her ideas of right and wrong seemed to lie the fault."

" Her knowledge of right and wrong ! That woman is one of Dr. Willard's prominent members, — a pious and exemplary woman ! "

" She does n't give him much credit for his teaching, and it is to be hoped there are not many who follow her example. It is to be deplored that so many religious people so demean their religion by their every-day behavior."

"You will find out how many there are before you have been in business many years. I have some curiosity to see how your high-flown theories will come out. You've got your store and yourself to support, and you must make up for such customers in some way, if you do it out of others."

Aye, aye! suggested the inner. That is one of the tricks of trade. Profits are averaged. What is lost on one another is compelled to make up. That is rather a one-sided interpretation of justice! It must require a very nice calculation to assess those profits if it is done accurately; but I strongly suspect that those who trade in that way give a large margin for incidental entries.

"It is true one couldn't support a store long on such custom as hers. And I see very clearly the difficulty of working reformation in such people. The whole, in their own opinion, need not a physician."

"Her kind of religion is contemptible. I've no patience with it!"

"It is best to be charitable, and charge her short-comings to natural proclivities, and the lack of religion to conquer them. 'Out of the abundance of the heart the mouth speaketh.' Her heart was full of selfish calculation, and she acted it out. If she had practiced the dissimulation in concealing her motives that she did in tracking her milliner, she would n't have exposed the rottenness which lay in the inside of her whited sepulchre."

"Whited sepulchre! you 've given her the right name. It took you some time to get through the whitewash, and find out what was underneath. You will learn to distinguish them at a glance when you 've been in business awhile. And if your tongue don't strip off some of the whitewash I don't understand you."

"I try to do my duty to my fellow-woman, and I hope I shall continue to do so. I really intended the questions, that I put to the one that just went out, to be suggestive of improvement if she had chosen so to interpret them; but she did n't appreciate my teaching."

"It was because your teaching lacked point. If I had sent her out of the store, she would have understood."

III.

I AM conscious that I am in a captious mood to-night, a continuation of the frame of mind I have •been in all day.

It is possible that our own frame of mind gives coloring to the circumstances that surround us, and the opinions we form of the acts of others. It is not only possible, but probable; not only probable, but that is just the state of the case. I have seen examples of it in others, and I have experienced it in myself.

I have heard many a person applaud a sentiment one day, and condemn it the next; approve an act in one, and censure the same thing in another. The conclusion to be arrived at, in view of both acts was, plainly, that the opinion formed did not depend upon the sentiment or act, abstractly considered, but upon the state of the eyes through which it was viewed, or the ears upon which it sounded.

I have noticed that an object which was interesting and agreeable to me one day became tiresome and disgusting another without any apparent change in the object. On discussing the matter with the inner dual I found that some untoward event, such as disappointed efforts in some direction, an undigested

dinner, a sleepless night, or some other trifle, had
placed the concave for the convex glass before my
sight, or *vice versa,* so that my perception had become disturbed when I looked at the object.

This rule may safely be applied to the various
things which go to make up this terrestrial condition.
The question resolves itself into the view which the
individual dual takes of them.   Why the individual
should take so many-sided views of the same thing,
and why the many-sided views resolve themselves
into a one-sided view, and why the constant effort of
the one-sided view is to exalt and exonerate itself at
the expense of antagonistic views, can be explained
only on one principle.

That principle is an axiom to the initiated.   It
consists in the entire devotion of the dual to the individual, and the responsive, tender, and devoted attachment of the individual to the dual self; therefore, what goes to depreciate the compound individual in his own eyes is to be eschewed.

Talking of axioms, another presents itself in
connection with this.   It is that every one likes to
appear to the best possible advantage in the eyes of
those with whom he associates.   These two axioms
established, it follows that what goes to depreciate
the individual in the eyes of the dual and his associates, makes the compound human uncomfortable
throughout his whole inner existence.   Therefore,
the profound humiliation in his own eyes that follows conviction of a fault is so disagreeable to be

borne that it has become a universal habit of human
duality to shift all wrong as speedily as possible
upon circumstances, or outside individuals. Hence
the many ingenious devices called into action to
create many-sided views which resolve themselves
perpetually into one-sided views.

If I appear ill-natured in the remarks I make
concerning the customer upon whom I have conferred the distinction of my particular notice to-day,
it may be attributed to the east wind, or her especial
deserts; not at all to my state of mind.

A mincing little Miss came caracoling up to the
counter where I stood, in search of materials for a
bonnet.

With the accumulated wit and wisdom of eighteen
summers upon her old-fashioned head she was fairly
out of leading-stings, mentally. Strange how the
mind agonizes itself into maturity in the verdant
spring-time of the manners!

The young lady had ventured to leave mamma at
home in charge of the family, and wended her
winding way into the labyrinths of trade.

Papa had intrusted her at starting with a five-
dollar bill, accompanied with the thrifty charge to
make it go as far as possible. I wish it to be understood that I do not affirm as to these proceedings at
home. The outer eye did not witness them. The
inner eyes, which are spiritual and penetrate to the
things of the spirit, caught up the inspiration of the
home scenes, and made record of them.

The young lady knew how to make good use of the supposititious teachings of the head of her family, as will be shown. Untaught nature could hardly have suggested the artifice she practiced to get her bonnet cheap.

She wriggled and twisted, advanced and retreated, curvetted and pranced, till finally she arrived where I stood, and lisped out, —

" Show me some buff flowers, if you please."

I showed her some of a soft, mellow tinge. She asked the price. They were imported flowers, and -expensive. I saw her countenance darken when I told her, but she made no other sign as to the price. She looked at them a moment longer ; then, with an air of importance which only the possession of a five-dollar bank note can confer, said, —

" Those are too light."

Verily it was spoken with the assumed air that it was a ten-dollar bill. How should a saleswoman be supposed to know that it was only a five? With proper management she might be impressed that it was ten, or twenty even.

The saleswoman suspected the *ruse,* and I'll reveal in due time how she knew all about it to a certainty.

I showed her some a little darker.

"Those are too dark !" with the same air.

I showed her every variety of shade which we had.

"I don't like any of them ;" she lisped out, with a

toss of her little head, and a shrug of her little shoulders.

I saw that she was n't in to buy; but I went on to show her the laces and ribbons that she asked for. Some were too light, some too dark, some too red, some too yellow, all were too something to suit.

Here was another whited sepulchre. The wash was put on thin, in the measure of the money in her pocket. Perhaps experience was educating my vision. I penetrated her purpose, but I pitied the little hypocrite. I considered that she was more sinned against than sinning. She was practicing what she had been taught. Therefore with Christian, or Job-like patience I kept my temper. Poor little thing! so young in years, so old in guile! I helped her along, — as the sun shines on the evil and the good? Certainly! is not that the way a Christian should do? I made no manifestation but that I thought she was making a praiseworthy effort to fulfill her father's injunction.

I saw that she was in to see what kind of goods were in use, and learn their prices so as to cheapen them in the next store.

After listening to my representations of what colors and combinations would be pretty for her, she said, with unnumbered, expressive little tosses of her head, —

"I don't think I 'll order a bonnet, after all — I think I 'll buy one all made," and she passed on into the saloon. Another half hour was spent in looking at made bonnets.

I noticed that she did not examine them with an eye to their abstract beauty, or to their appropriateness for her. She investigated the manner of their construction with the careful study of an artist intending to copy. Then, she became transparent; I saw through her to the bottom. She was going to make her own bonnet, and was making herself mistress of the way to do it by a careful examination of ours. She was helping herself gratuitously to the benefit of skill which had been bought and paid for.

I was not angry with the little thief; my indignation spent itself in another direction. Shame on the training that had brought forth such fruits from such a soil! The inner dual saw down into the depths of the cultivation that had matured such fruit. The dressing and sub-plowing, the furrowing, and putting in of the seed, and the daily tending, the watering and nurturing that made it grow.

I longed to take that child away from the atmosphere in which she had so thriven, and show her how meanly and wickedly she was behaving. Did her sin lie at her own door?

After completing her inspection, she said, with one grand flourish, the culminated air in which was mingled the doubly refined, highly concentrated, compound extract of all her former airs, —

"I don't find any thing that exactly suits me; I won't purchase to-day. I know I'm awful particular, but I can't help it."

The possession of that five-dollar note had given her an edifying consciousness of her own importance. If she went out with the idea that she had impressed me that she was a young lady of such fastidious · taste that so ordinary an exhibition of pretty things had failed to satisfy it, she entirely mis· apprehended the state of my mentals.

I pitied her for a silly little thing of airs and pretences; but not quite so shallow as she appeared on the surface. She had depth enough to plan and perform quite a little *rôle* in order to get her bonnet cheap. If she acted it to her own' satisfaction, alas for its execution upon me!

My capacity to penetrate was quite equal to hers for originating and executing her sham.

Sham! yes, sham! It is the rule of action in the outer life. One motive is put forward while another and a very different from that on exhibition is what really actuates in the transaction performed. When a man really wishes to buy an article, he puts on an air of indifference toward it; he often goes further and depreciates it with words. These tactics are carried into all the transactions and acts of life, till sincerity itself is often put on as a trap.

Silly fools! We act as though the keen vision of equally alert shammers were not wide open, staring down into and compassing every thought that stirs in our inner chamber.

What a world of humiliation we might save ourselves if we would recognize, remember, and act

upon the fact that others are as apt to scrutinize
our motives, and are as capable of doing it as we
theirs.   Sincerity would certainly be induced out of
shame, — a result which principle rarely accom-
plishes.

To act sincerely would not always save us from
the uncharitable judgments of others.   Our acquaintances judge of us as they are in themselves.
They construe our acts, be they never so sincere,
according to their own one-sided interpretation, and
it often proves that they judge far off the truth.
That is one of the crosses of the flesh to be borne
patiently till we see eye to eye, when the misappre-
hension will be rectified.

But to act sincerely would obtain our own self-
respect, which is an ennobling end to attain.   A
consciousness of rectitude makes a man, or woman,
stand upright, and look the world in the face, un-
dauntedly, however much it may scowl.

To act sincerely is to obtain the approbation of
the Father, a consideration well worth the whole
effort of the united human dual.

Another benefit, worth mentioning, would accrue
from sincerity in intercourse with our fellows.   Cause
of offence not being given, the sins of the unruly
member would be diminished to the pacification of
the wicked feuds that now disfigure the face of many
a Christian community, — feuds which cause the
finger of " the world's people " to be pointed thereat,
and the shout to sound out, Fie ! for shame !

Sincerity in action would prolong the existence of the mortal strata of the dual indefinitely beyond the allotted longevity of three score and ten, — if he could only be persuaded to test the quality of such a physical preservative.

The wear and tear of perplexities, anxieties, and manual labor that shamming imposes upon the dual, consumes vitality in ruinous ratio to the amount of happiness, which is life, that it confers. How many, that indefinite length of days might become if sincerity were to be the rule of life, I lack the means of demonstrating, and I have serious apprehensions that human statistics will always labor under such destitution.

I saw my customer go into the next store. I had occasion to go there also on an errand of my own. Probably I had no design to follow her, and see what use she made of the knowledge she had just acquired from me. *I* is not one of the shammers; the offensive *U* is always the offending party.

I followed her, and stood beside the counter while she made her purchases. It is necessary to have rules in trade that will work both ways. We must follow up, and find out the character of our customers, so as not to waste time and attention upon those who don't pay us. If we are watched we return the compliment by watching. I saw that she followed my suggestions about her materials.

On every article she got off a few cents by telling the saleswoman that she could get them a little cheaper at our place, in which statement she usually transgressed the truth.

By her manœuvre she got the materials for her bonnet "very reasonably." And, no doubt, she so boasted to her thrifty sire when he investigated her financiering after she arrived home. And no doubt her skill in making profitable investments received its due meed of approbation. The inner dual followed her home, saw her exhibit her purchases, tell what we asked for just such things, and how much cheaper she got them. It saw the wink of recognition that passed between the parents as her shrewdness vaunted itself, and the caressing pat of laudation conferred upon the smirking little cheek.

The spirit is an unlimited traveller.

If I had the meting out of retributions, the course of discipline which I would mark out for that young woman would be, to compel her to invest that five-dollar note in millinery. Then, I would compel her to wait upon such customers as she was to me till her five dollars had earned her a bonnet in her profits. Can any mathematician tell me how long she would go bareheaded?

I don't object to the girl making her own bonnet, if she does so honestly. It was the filching of our time and skill that was objectionable. One who has little or no practice may be able to make a tolerable bonnet, but the touch which a milliner inscribes upon her handiwork is wanting. Unpracticed hands, however Nature may have endowed them with skill, can never impart the ease and elegance of finish which characterize cultivated aptness.

There is no such thing as genius without knowledge. Aptness will succeed with less than stupidity.

A man may be a born lawyer, but he must study statutes before he can practice successfully.

A man may be a born doctor, but he must learn the science of medicine, and its application to the physique before he can become skillful in curing diseases. Nature may bend the mind to suit a vocation, but diligent application to learn the details which constitute it is necessary in order to perfect one in the use of it.

A little knowledge may serve one's purpose, but after the trouble and expense of education has been at by others, those who require the little, if they take it from those who have purchased the much, ought to pay for it. An ounce of knowledge should be paid for as much as the pound.

It would be equally just and reasonable to expect a lawyer to give you the benefit of his legal knowledge, or a doctor his medical services without return for value received, as to take advantage of acquired millinery skill without payment.

The sin of quackery is its deception. Its popularity is not based upon its superior merits, but its availability. Its knowledge of human nature insures its success. The hook is baited with an advertise-

ment of cheapness. Who can resist a nibble? Not
those whose first, second, and last consideration, is
the "almighty dollar."

Almighty is no surreptitious appellation to confer
on the lustrous ore stamped with man's image.
Omnipotent is its rule, and omnipresent its consideration. Where does it not take precedence of
the durable riches of righteousness?

Cheapness is paramount to taste, fitness, or durability. The seekers for cheapness have their reward.
The abiding qualities of the articles they buy are
transient in ratio of money spent for them.

IV.

WE had an illustration to-day of quack millinery, and its saving qualities. Too much of the salt of economy may prove as destructive to the purse as too little.

Last week a lady came in to get a bonnet pressed over, saying that she had trimmings at home, and that a friend who had trimmed her own would put it on for her. As an excuse for so doing, she remarked, — " It costs so much to get a bonnet trimmed · nowadays."

To-day she brought it back, with her trimming, to have it fitted up. Her friend had tried on it two or three times, and failed to suit.

The unskillful hands had injured the bonnet so much that we were obliged to incur the expense of returning it to the bleachery to have it pressed again. So much for the saving part of the operation.

We took every pains to make up for this disappointment because she treated us like a lady.

She told us honestly when she first brought the bonnet what she intended to do. When she brought it back, she was just as frank in representing her foolishness, as she called it, in trying to save in the wrong place. I record for the edification of those who think like her, and the instruction of those who have n't had her experience, or are not so sensible, the remarks she made when she gave me the bonnet back.

"It is better to let all trades live. My husband is a physician, he practices and has his pay, and it is the proper thing for us to pay back his earnings to those that employ him by employing them in their particular business. I was too greedy in trying to save out of you, and he told me so when I showed him my bonnet this morning."

I liked her, and I led her to talk on.

"Every one has not a particular calling through which to receive back what they pay out."

. "They ought to have," she replied quickly. "If you knew how much disease is caused by idleness you would indorse the remark. The necessity of work is the salvation of health."

"Still if one does work and earn, it is proper to save all he can," I remarked.

"Certainly," she replied, "I save in the right place by wearing my last summer trimming. It may not be so desirable as a new one, but it answers every purpose on a bonnet which I wish to wear only·when I go out on business, for a drive, or the like."

"There are circumstances where it would be impossible for one to be engaged in regular employment," I pursued.

" Yes, but those cases are rare ; they are the exceptions. It is usually false pride, or indolence, that prompts people to live in idleness ; especially those that sponge their living out of others. There ought to be a law that every child, male or female, should learn some trade or profession, so that they could get their living. If parents have n't sense to see what is for their good, I would have the State take the education of children in hand, as it did in olden times."

" But if they were not disposed to follow it after they were taught ? " I asked.

" I would have that in the law, that they should do so if they were not disposed."

" Some are disposed to make all they can out of their own occupation and that of others too," I remarked.

" Yes," she replied with an arch look ; " and yours is not the only trade which that class of people are disposed to take advantage of. We are sponged as well as you. Many and many a woman has come to me, and asked in a friendly way, what I do for myself and my children when we are affected so and so, instead of going to my husband for advice, and paying for it. I have been thoroughly disgusted with such meanness ; and my husband told me this morning that I had been doing the same thing by you, and I felt ashamed ; but I hope I have made amends."

I could have taken that woman in my arms, and

hugged her. I did take her to the inner dual, and
lay her on my heart, as a healing balm for the wound
that the little hypocrite of yesterday made. I had
entertained an angel, and her visit was as refreshing
as if from the presence of the Lord.

I don't know what church she belongs to, I don't
know if she is a professor of religion, but if I could
I would send this act as a memorial of her down to
all coming generations.

I was telling my landlady at tea to-night the
incident here recorded, and she remarked in her
grave way — " I was just as mean as that once, but I
did n't know it till I went into a store to 'tend. My
eyes were then opened, I was convicted, and I hope
converted from the error of my ways. I never go into
a store now without considering that there are two
parties whose interests are to be consulted in making a trade. Some buy to better advantage than
others on account of the state of the market, or from
having more means to do so, and on that account
can afford to sell for less. I think it is right to go
where I can do best for myself; but to lie and deceive in order to get an article cheaper is just as
contemptible in a customer as in a trader. Some
traders are disposed to take advantage of you, and
the way to treat them is to let them alone severely."

She was quite out of breath when she got through
with her speech. It was rather a long one to deliver
in the way of colloquy. But my landlady is a grand

woman. The more I see of her, the better I like her.

Question : If tending store has such a wonderful effect upon the moral element of the human dual, why would n't it be well, as a normal exercise, for Sabbath-school teachers, to take a salutary course of training in that fitting department during the secular days of the week?

I am not sure — this is only the opinion of one humble person — that ministers would n't gain more available information of the real characters of their hearers, wherefrom to preach adaptive and instructive sermons, by a course of observations in a store, in a week, than they now obtain in a lifetime of parochial parlor visits and vestry conferences.

Parishioners usually feel it incumbent on them to dress their manners in Sunday garb, and sit in state, with toes turned out and heels turned in, when their minister makes his appearance. Their language must also be arranged after the rules of grammatical syntax, perfumed with the strongest extract of righteousness.

When engaged in making a trade minor considerations are forgotten, the one great object becomes absorbing ; and the ruling passion crops out with a luxuriance unknown to the chilly atmosphere of conventional vegetation. Those ministers ambitious of a reputation for smartness, who like to point a home-thrust by witty exposition, and gratify their hearers, or their vanity, by displaying their keenness, could hardly find more suggestive or useful hints for their purposes than those furnished in a store. Dull must be the blade of satire that is n't ground to dissecting sharpness on the whetstone of bargaining.

V.

I AM located in business with the great question of, What is honesty? yet unsettled, although I have been perplexing myself with it night and day for the last six months.

A very simple question it might seem to one not involved in the intricacies of business, but once let one get entangled in the mazes of buying and selling, and it would be beyond the ingenuity of a lawyer to extricate his ideas of honesty.

I resolved myself into a committee of the whole upon the aforementioned question, and have been gravely sitting upon it — by no means so easy a seat as to make satisfactory accommodations — during this tedious length of time, to no purpose. The longer I have sat, the harder has grown the seat, and more mystifying has grown the problem. It opens and shuts to my understanding, like a showery day, but chiefly shuts.

" Honesty is the best policy." How easy it is to propound proverbs!

What is honesty? The answer has been pharaphrased into innumerable platitudes, but nothing practically satisfactory has yet been educed from it. It is evident that the paraphrasts have never been in trade. How can they understand that words strung together to make grandiloquent fulminations ill compare with the little actions which must be strung together, through a lifetime, to make a telling practice?

My solution of honesty has n't yet transpired, but the policy upon which I start is decided. I will keep a good quality of goods, and do my best to please those who favor me with their custom. If I do that I must be paid for it. I must be judge, not my customers, how large profits will suffice to pay me, and who is best able to pay them.

One point I have settled in my own mind beyond a cavil, and the conclusion has been reached from the facts which my eyes have revealed to my understanding.

The naked truth is, that people go to buy goods with one unadulterated purpose in their thoughts, and that is, to buy just as advantageously to themselves as possible, without the slightest interest whether the seller makes or loses through their custom. I am a little too fast. Many appear very much exercised with doubts and fears lest a trader should make something out of them; but as to the losses of the tradesman customers manifest a wonderful resignation to the allotments of Providence.

At this point another popular proverb may be inserted with peculiar adaptation to the subject. "It is a poor rule that won't work both ways." In view of the proceedings of customers, why may not a trader be allowed to look, in unique calculation, at his own interest.

Thence arises the question, What is for my interest, and how shall I best advance it? I wish to secure a good class of customers. What is a good customer? One who has plenty of money, and is willing to spend it for what he wants. At any rate, he must be willing to spend his own, or that of some one else. If he wishes to spend he will find a way to get. How? That is asking one question beyond the province of a tradesman to understand. To know that a customer has money, and is willing to spend it, and does spend it in paying for his goods, ought to suffice the curiosity of a person who has goods to sell.

That kind of a customer takes the rank of general, commanding the whole army of customers, — in goodness? That depends upon the rendering of the word goodness. If it is rendered a financial quality, yes. If a moral or social adjunct, various modification might be introduced.

As an illustration of the socially good customer, here comes Mrs. Tallmadge, stately and serene as a military monument, "tight-fisted" as a contribution offertory in the vestibule of a Roman Catholic Church; which depository of money for the poor, or the priest, is made with one narrow opening on top by which coins can gain access, but having no visible outlet whereby they may find egress. She has a great deal of social influence, a ready will where she takes, and a fluent tongue to make it available. Therefore I wish to secure her custom.

Where shines the light of her aristocratic countenance, there beam the light-giving rays of her train of followers. What mayor's lady has not her admirers; leastwise, while she is lady mayoress. If a part of the admiration she receives belongs, rightly distributed, to the office her husband represents, and the honor his partner shares, what is that to us? It is not with her honors, or the admiration, in consequence of possession, bestowed upon her, that we have to do. It is singly and solely of the benefit that is to accrue to us from having her custom, and that of her train of admirers, that we speak.

Her solitary custom would starve a church mouse, but the set she leads are not all so sharp as she. They take her representation so far as cheapness is concerned. All are very respectable, and will give a good name to my establishment.

Mrs. Tallmadge is a strong-minded lady mayoress, and has instituted a protective office, in her own independent right, commensurate with that of her husband's; the difference being that her husband's is of a civil, and hers of a social character.

She has constituted herself the guardian of all the purses of her acquaintances against the abuses of tradespeople.

She goes around to all the stores in town, compares the quality of the different stocks, and the prices, and then reports them through the circle of her acquaintance. The one who sells cheapest has the benign influence of her sanction. She trades with him, and advises every one she knows to do the same.

It is impossible to deceive her, the ruling passion keeps itself healthy and vigorous by unflagging exercise. . Although she is lady mayoress now, she was in trade once, and can't rid herself of the odor of a tradeswoman. She perfumes up every time she makes a shopping expedition, and distributes distilled sweets through her notability and shrewdness wherever she goes afterwards.

She is a philanthropist in active, enterprising operation. In the exercise of her disinterested benevolence she advises her friends, solely for their own good, to trade only at the places where they can buy to the best advantage. The result to be obtained by such a course is to keep down the price of goods to a reasonable amount.

If one is disposed to undersell, she protects him from the anger of his fellow tradespeople by her august dictum that he has a right to do as he pleases. He is trading on the policy of making small profits and quick turns.

She came in to-day, and if there is one article in the store that she did n't examine, and as a necessary concomitant, ask the price of, it has escaped my memory.

In leaving, she stated to me her own experience, and advised me to follow it. Here she had an opportunity to exercise her philanthropy to my advantage.

4

"If I were you," she said, "I would sell cheap till I got my name up. Then, after you have got a good run of custom, you can rise in your prices."

. She, of course, had no interest in advising me to such a course of policy. She was interested in my welfare, and desirous to see me get a good start in business. The inner dual in presenting the case to her view argued, that as success was to be for my benefit, the means to attain it ought to be at my expense. This advice added another complex section to my chapter on honesty. Maybe such a policy might draw custom, but methinks as soon as I raised my prices my customers would consider themselves wronged, and leave for the benefit of some other new store. And it might be for their supposed interest to misrepresent me for the wrong I had done them. It may be honesty to follow the advice, but I am skeptical as to the policy.

I replied, " By selling cheaper than others I shall get their ill-will, and so long as I am situated among them that would make me unhappy."

" You might as well dispense with such silly notions if you are going to remain in trade, and battle for yourself. They will pay no such regard to your feelings. You will be sure of their ill-will if you get custom."

I said no more. If she congratulated herself that she had silenced my scruples it was all one to me. She had the comfort of thinking her superior wisdom had enlightened me. I saw it was my wisdom not to reduce the quantity of her self-esteem by appearing to differ in opinion from her.

The inner dual gently suggested, if you get their ill-will without cause it can be borne. If you do what brings it upon you, you have nothing to sustain you.

I wished to secure her good-will if not her custom, so I was all smiles and attention. The smiles were not always the complacent cordiality they expressed, but they answered every purpose. They were graciously accepted. I ached under the attention shockingly, because I saw some ladies, that I knew came to buy if I had what suited them, go out of the store because I was engaged. I bore it as patiently as I could, comforting myself with the reflection that if she lost me something in custom she would save me money in advertising. In that selfish consideration I became entirely oblivious of the interests of the "poor printer." I beg his pardon. I am obliged, in common parlance, to look out for Number One at the risk of overlooking my friends.

I thanked her for her interest in my success, which her advice and other proceedings indicated, hoped she would favor me with another visit, and courtesied her to the door with the greatest pleasure.

Was I hypocritical? By no means! only politic. There is great emphasis in the proverb, "The truth is n't to be told at all times." Does that teaching imply that a lie may be told sometimes? It seems merely to involve another equally trite and popular dogma? "A wise head keeps a close mouth."

But supposing a lie is effected by keeping back a part of the truth? Shade of Solomon! how questions multiply if you once commence the study of morals. They follow each other like a fourth of July procession, and tire the conscience as the pedestrian display pains the foot.

If I retain a part of the truth from communication, as I did in the case of Mrs. Tallmadge, and if from that concealment she infer that I am perfectly delighted with her, and all of her sentiments, where rests the fault of the wrong inference? With Mrs. Tallmadge, I insist, understanding all the bearings of the case upon my interests. If she knew the whole truth, which event I hope may never transpire, she would undoubtedly take a very different view of it. In the nervous excitement produced by the wound inflicted upon her self-esteem, she would summarily pronounce the sentence of hypocrite upon me, and charge me with having deceived her. Which charge I should repel by the accusation that she had deceived herself. Criminations and recriminations might follow very much to the detriment of good morals and good manners.

In practical solution that is a wise proverb which writeth for our instruction, "The truth should n't be told at all times."

Mrs. Tallmadge has, in her own eyes, performed a wonderful *coup-de-main* in order to get her bonnet and little fineries cheap. Perhaps she is smarter than I am, but if it is within the pale of female ingenuity, a pale that incloses a large circumference, to devise means to make her a profitable customer, I propose to accomplish that laudable result.

She has the means, and it is perfectly proper that she should pay for the trouble she makes. It is none of my plan to put my face on her whetstone; and then, to turn and grind out of some aping simpleton who has no such worldly wisdom, the profit which that old, meddlesome poor-grinder ought to pay.

"A bird that can sing and won't sing, must be made to sing," is another, and very interesting proverb, which makes a very pertinent practical application to the Tallmadge discourse.

I will endeavor to convince that woman that she is getting extraordinary things at extraordinary prices.

This very day I have set the girls at work upon a bonnet that is to be the only one of the kind imported this season. I know I can hit off her complexion and form of features to a charm. I had plenty of time to study her while she was rummaging over my goods.

I have ordered a wooden box, because French bonnets come in wooden boxes, and I will Frenchify it off with pictures and French printing, so that the box can help along the story.

Let me see! black as Hagar! Where did that

phrase come from? Tradition must be the mother
of it. If Hagar mothers the African race she is not
Mrs. Tallmadge's foremother, but the next thing to
it. There is no blond blood in her complexion.
Scarlet shades and black, no pale reds, but just a bit
of white, — that will do, I was right. The scarlet
next the face, to throw some color on the cheeks.
That long, narrow face; — it won't do to pile the
flowers on top as they do now. I must have them
down a bit at the side to broaden the forehead, and
draw the white spray over the front of the bonnet.
Yes, I have it.

Mrs. Tallmadge shall try that bonnet when she
comes in again, and she shall buy that bonnet, and
her purse shall remunerate the officers of the customs
for all the trouble they have taken about it.

That woman is supposed to be made in God's own
image. It must be in regard to the general appearance. In the details of construction she may as
fairly be supposed to differ.

When Mrs. Tallmadge went out, silly little Mrs.
Flaunty was passing. Seeing her mayoress-ship
making her egress, she rushed with all the speed
that curiosity could hasten to the saleswoman that
stood nearest the door.

"Did Mrs. Tallmadge buy her bonnet here?" she
asked in breathless eagerness.

The girl directed her to me to gratify her curiosity. Here was an opportunity to turn Mrs. Tallmadge to advantage. Putting on a reticent air I
answered, —

" I think she will buy her bonnet here."

I really thought she would. Indeed it was my fixed purpose to draw her into such an arrangement. And if Mrs. Flaunty was drawn by force of example to do the same thing, I should sell two bonnets instead of one.

" What is she going to have ? " pursued the eager questioner. " Can I see it ? "

" I never show a customer's bonnet, even to her best friends. Many ladies would be offended if I were to do so. You will see her bonnet when she wears it."

" You are real lucky to get her custom," said little Flaunty ; " she will tell everybody who made her bonnet."

I assented with a smile.

" I must come here one of these days and get mine, when Flaunty fills my purse," she said.

I internally commented, When you have seen Mrs. Tallmadge's. What will you do if you don't succeed with Tallmadge? suggested caution. She will think Tallmadge has changed her mind, — one of the most common events to happen in a woman's life, and always to be safely presumed upon.

Flaunty is a subject to make a good trade out of. She has n't one particle of. Tallmadge's shrewdness or knowledge. She will believe any thing I tell her, since she thinks my lady mayoress is my patron. My lady's notability is as far-famed as her distinguished person is known. Where is the lady mayoress who does not enjoy the like notoriety? More than that, where is there a lady mayoress who does n't labor under, if she does n't rejoice in, a reputation for characteristics of which she never dreamed, conferred by *Vox populi*.

It is safe for any one to trade where Mrs. Tallmadge does, and very desirable, Mrs. Flaunty would argue.

Shall I impose upon the little simpleton? Shade of honesty! no! If I put a trick upon any one it shall be on an equal, and never upon her unless she attempts to play off on me first. I think it is right to play back in such a case. I should as soon think of taking advantage of a child as of Flaunty. Her husband is an honest, hard-working man, and supplies his wife with all the money he can spare, and that is by no means a superabundance. He loves her, and delights to see her gratify her taste in dress.

Flaunty will trust me. Would I deceive a person that trusts me? God forbid! Let my right hand forget her cunning when I make a dishonest bonnet for an honest woman.

VI.

IT turns out as I calculated. My urbanity to the Right Honorable Mrs. Tallmadge has brought her round again, only a little sooner than I expected.

There are some distinguished strangers in town. The mayor is to dine them, and Madam desired a new head-dress under which to honor the occasion, so she said.

If she came to pass away the time that intervenes before she can exhibit her graces before those who can carry the fame thereof into more remote neighborhoods than she had as yet been spread over, it was right for me to improve it for my own benefit, and I did so.

She would give no directions at all about the cap. " Make me one suitable to my age and station," was her order. I selected the materials, and set the girls at work to make up an age-and-station cap. I knew well enough about her station, but how to fit a cap to it! Direct me, my guardian angel, so that I make no blunder! Her age, I would n't dare hazard a guess upon it in her hearing for fear of giving offense ; but I thought I could hit it in her cap. If I made a mistake, on the verdant side, of two or three years, no exceptions would be taken.

While the age-and-station cap was in progress, I thought I might as well be advancing my plans about the French bonnet.

I fortified my purpose with the consideration that she was lawful game. I gave her taste, and knowledge of the quality of goods many a pointed compliment while we were talking, — her palate for such condiments was n't delicate, — till I put her in perfect good-humor with herself, and of course with me.

I have observed, and there is profound policy inclosed in the fact if one is disposed to study it out and reduce it to practice, that the better pleased a woman is with herself the better the feelings which she will manifest toward all the rest of the world. *Ergo*, the more self-satisfied you can make a woman in your store, the better satisfied she will be with you. The more pleased she is with you, the better she will like your bonnets; the better satisfied she is with your bonnets, the more likely she will be to buy them, and pay your prices without grumbling.

I was very careful to tell Mrs. Tallmadge the price of her cap a little more than I intended it should amount to when it was done. To take off something in the price was a convincing argument with her that she got an article "reasonable."

I knew my woman, and I knew if I asked her twenty-five cents for an article, she would want it for twelve. If I asked her twelve, she would want it for six. If I asked her six, she would want it for nothing. If I gave it to her, she would want me to pay her something for taking it.

I took pains that the age-and-station cap should be becoming, and equally as much pains to impress it upon her mind that it was so. I contrived to compliment her on the points in her looks upon which I saw that she prided herself.

Being pleased with herself, the cap, and the unpresuming recorder of this event, I found little difficulty in arranging matters with her purse.

I'll state how I managed that matter of price in order that it may stimulate my memory if I fall upon similar circumstances again when I am in a quandary about honesty, and don't know how to act.

In the first place I showed her each article separately, and asked her to judge of the value, always cautioning her to remember the rise in the price of goods, and to judge of mine by the rise in other things. In that way I let her set her own price, which was usually more than mine. If she fell short I added a little, but not enough to make her feel that she had committed an error. Or, I made an apology, that it could n't be expected she could keep the run of every little thing when prices were so fluctuating; I could n't do it myself.

In the exercise of her vaunted shrewdness, if she had seen my reckoning when it was cast up, she might have congratulated herself that she paid me a little over a dollar more than I would have thought of asking her if left in the exercise of my unbiased honesty.

When she got through with her head-dress, I said to her in a low, confidential tone, —

"I have something new and very desirable in the way of bonnets to show you in my private room."

She followed me eagerly, with the mother Eve propensity glittering in her two eyes, and breathing through her parted lips.

I showed her my imported bonnets, and expatiated largely on the beauties of the one I designed for her especial adornment. I explained to her how admirably the colors and form were adapted to her style and complexion. I told her it came high, being imported, — so it was, every item, even the sewing-silk with which it was made. I told her I did n't expect to make any thing, scarcely a living, the first year, and I carelessly remarked, " You understand why?" I did n't say I was following her advice to sell cheap; if she inferred that I intended to it was her own voluntary act.

"I presume I do," was the self-satisfied answer.

"Prices may become an object with ladies in your position, in these times," I said, insinuating that generally they were supposed, owing to their social elevation, to be above caring for such trifles. She did n't take the hint I gave her bump of calculation in the way I intended, but quickly answered, —

"Certainly; the price is a very important th'ng."

Instead of mustering pride to my aid, I had stirred up the ruling passion to oppose me. I made a sudden move, and without much reconnoitring pitched upon a more salient point. It takes a woman to understand the quicksands of a woman's vanity. I stretched my net in more shallow waters. I was bent on hitting, even at the risk of loss; so I said with one of my blandest smiles, which was intended to add to the comeliness of my countenance, and by my insinuating manners I endeavored to enforce the suggestion I was making, —

" It is quite proper, indeed it is absolutely necessary, when ladies are getting toward middle life, that they should pay a little extra attention to their dress, even at the expense of what may appear to be a little extravagance."

I knew she must be much nearer sixty than forty; but to remind her of her age without a compliment attached, as a bait, would have been ruinous to my purpose. To remind her that she was getting along in years, and needed all the advantages which dress could bestow was the most favorable motive I could arouse in favor of disposing of my bonnet.

" You might try it on, and see the effect," I suggested. I was almost certain, if she tried its effect, that she would be unwilling to deny herself its advantages.

" That can do no harm; " and in a moment more it triumphantly crowned her imperial head. There is no misuse of language in that expression. When her husband was elected mayor she became a princess of the blood in the American code of royalty. Triumphant I knew the bonnet was at the first glance she gave herself in the mirror.

" What is the price ? " she asked directly.

I hesitated a moment, and then told her as much
as I dared venture.   I had no conscientious scruples
against taking all I could get; but a little apprehension arose in my mind that her saving propensities
would receive so great a shock as to defeat my purpose.   She continued to look at herself for several
moments in rapt admiration, the inner dual was im-
pudent enough to. say distinctly to itself, but the
outer lips remarked, —

"That bonnet relieves you of ten years of your
age."

"I think it is becoming.   If I conclude to take it
you will abate something on the price?"

"As it is you, I suppose I must, a trifle."

I did n't say, or intend to convey the idea, that it
was out of personal esteem that I would take something off the price.   Neither did I think it necessary
to state, in order to be sincere, that I would take it
off because, owing to her character, that was the better way to get on with her.

After studying upon it awhile, she said, " I 'm not
in the habit of committing such an extravagance
as to buy a French bonnet, but this one takes my
fancy.   Could n't you get me up one just like it, and
make it come a little cheaper?"

"It would be difficult for us to give it the real
French style which characterizes this.   And *you*
would n't want an imitation, — nothing short of the
genuine would satisfy *you*."

That was just the argument to use.   A genuine

article was her delight.   To be imposed upon with a
spurious one aroused her strongest indignation.

" Well, how much will you take off? "

I told her.   Still she hesitated.

" I was n't intending to buy to-day."

" It may be gone," I suggested.   " My profits being small, I am obliged to hurry my sales ; — that is
why I sell so cheap."   I was in a hurry to sell her
the bonnet.

" Has any one seen it ? "

" No.   It came in last night, and you are the first
lady who has been in that I thought would care for
so nice a bonnet."

" Perhaps I might as well take it.   I don't think,
if I should go the whole town over, that I could find
any thing to suit me better ; but I might find something cheaper."

I thought that I would snap that bubble, although
I saw that the bonnet was sold.

" You might find something, but if you bought a
cheaper, it would n't look like this.   And every time
you put it on your head you would say to yourself,
How foolish I was to buy a dowdy bonnet for the
sake of saving a few dollars ! "

A dowdy bonnet! horror of horrors! what lady
could endure the thought and survive !

She was equal to me.   " I shall think of my extravagance every time I put this on."

" But you will be able to offset that unpleasant
reflection by the knowledge that you have what suits

you. If you pay for what suits you, there is some
comfort in it. You have got what is pretty and becoming, and a genuine article, so there is no money
wasted. But if you get a bonnet that don't suit, it is
all wasted. A little more spent when you are buying pays you in the comfort you take with it."

" I know I sha'n't be satisfied with any thing short
of this, now I have seen it," was her reply to that
argument ; " but I think I'll let it remain till I come
in again."

I did n't know whether she proposed that arrangement to gain time for reconsideration of her resolu-
tion to buy, or to make further opportunities to be
running in. Either way, I had no interest in helping her carry out her plan. If she reconsidered, and
looked around, some one might induce her to change
her mind. As she made her calls of " lengthened
sweetness long drawn out," their frequency was n't
particularly desirable. I suggested, —

" Some accident might happen to it. The girls
are always handling bonnets, and ladies that come
in are constantly trying them. If some one took a
fancy to it they might sell it when I am out. The
safer way would be to take it if you decide upon it.
It might get soiled, or sold."

" I have n't the money, with me, to pay for it."

" Never mind ; send it in any time."

The supposition of possible harm hit in the right
corner, just where her care-taking organ was located,
and the bonnet went into her carriage.

Victory! shouted the inner dual. It would have
been undignified to have made any outward demonstration. I have conquered the most obstinate case
of tight-fisted calculation in the whole town. I
have compassed the infinitesimal calculations of
that soul, and outwitted them.

The way I have managed her may seem unscru-
pulous to one ignorant of trade ; but I must manage
such people in some way, or they will manage me
into debt, and consequent dishonesty. It is better to
manage them so, than to come into collision with
them ; and quite as little violation of good morals is
involved.

There is no avail in grumbling ! There is quite
an amount of human nature displayed by most
women when they want a new bonnet, especially if
they have set their hearts on having it nice, and
pretty, and cheap at the same time. Not even my
unexceptional self is exempt from the imputation
of human fallibility included in the psychological
division of the affections which embrace the desire
to get gain without outlay. I trade where I can get
goods cheapest.

5

VII.

"I AM tired to death!" But it is the wholesome fatigue that insures sleep. I require no medicine to still my nerves. I go to bed, and go off soundly without a thought about it, and I am in the midst of a large boarding-house, and the rumble and rattle of the noisy streets.

I longed to tell my experience to some ladies who came in to-day. They sat a long time recounting their ails, and the number of physicians who had undertaken to cure them. In giving the pedigree of their diseases, I could n't fail to notice that they originated in having nothing to do but entertain themselves. That Mrs. Nothing-to-do has been a prolific mother of diseases, and Mrs. Imagination has been a successful dry-nurse in bringing them to maturity.

Pity it is their physicians have n't been honest enough to prescribe labor as a cure!

I told the girls that labor, steady, regular employment, is the only source of sound health and real comfort.

I told them they might congratulate themselves upon the appointment of their lot. The workers, with all their hardships, are happier than the idlers.

Exercise is necessary to promote growth in body and mind. All Nature verifies the law. The trees and grass must be exercised by the air, in order to healthy growth. They work constantly in appropriating their nourishment; unless they work they wither and die. Every leaf, every insect works. The air and the ocean work. I grew really eloquent upon the benefits of labor.

Gracie listened till I had exhausted myself, if not the topic; then she very modestly remarked, —

" But it is very hard to be obliged to work every day for one's living."

The idea she advanced struck me, it struck me so hard that it hurt me. I could not help assenting, although it injured my satisfactory apostrophe on the comeliness of labor.

" Yes, Gracie, " I said slowly, " you are right. But it is not the labor that is so hard, — it is the necessity to perform it. To be obliged to work or starve is a hard-faced necessity. To be obliged to work when it is considered a disgrace to do so is very hard. For a young girl to hang her head in shame because she is obliged to do what is right is harder still ; but it is a social state of things which Christians indorse, if they did not institute, and for which society is responsible."

I had delivered another nice thing : no doubt the girls thought, how beautifully she can talk; but the inner dual stirred round in an agony of deprecation.

What are you saying about the responsibility of society? Can society go to judgment in their banded perpetration of wrong to answer for the sins of a community? Nonsense! What are you saying about social responsibility? There are no commands in the Bible to society. I turned to Gracie again, and said humbly, —

"It is very wrong for any one to treat the fact of labor with disrespect, and much more so to treat one who labors so on that account. You are doing your duty nobly, in doing with your might what your hands find to do, and it is no matter how others regard you in consequence of it."

"But it is of consequence how one is regarded by others, and it is of great consequence whether one is poor or not. It would be difficult to convince me that it is n't pleasanter to be handsomely dressed, and ride around in a carriage, and have plenty of money to spend, and plenty of time to read and do what you like, than to be obliged to work all day for one's living, and be stinted for money, and dress meanly, and go on foot everywhere," said Gracie knowingly.

"The lot is cast into the lap, and the whole ordering thereof is of the Lord." We are not told what position in this life, or what worldly goods to strive to obtain. The Father has reserved the appointing of that to Himself; but He has told us how to behave if we are rich, and how to behave if we are poor. Our part is to submit; we must. We cannot resist the Hand that holds us; and it is our happiness to submit as good and obedient children. We shall know in the beyond why our appointment is one of labor, and that of others one of ease."

"I don't fret because I am obliged to work," she replied; "it would be of no use; I know that money is beyond my reach; but that don't make it any less desirable."

"It doubtless makes it more so. The unattainable is usually the most desirable in our eyes."

MAY 10, 18—.

What a stretching and straining there is among our ladies after the "Parisian." In consequence, how many camels do they ignorantly swallow. It is absolutely impossible to please without humbugging them. The taste for the far-fetched must be gratified, or one cannot succeed.

I am not responsible for the taste; I did n't create it. But you foster it by pandering to it. I cannot help it. The demand creates the supply. The supply cannot regulate the demand under ordinary circumstances. I am to comply with what the taste of my customers requires; I cannot regulate their tastes. If I thought them in error it would be a dangerous experiment for me to attempt to correct them. They would consider that I was setting my taste above theirs, and they would ignite at once in view of their own depreciation. We must take people as we find them, and make the best of them.

That little minikin-finnikin, Fannie Smith, has been in again about her flowers for the fourth time. She thought her flowers were not Parisian, — she was sure they were not real French, and she must have them changed.

" You like the flowers, do you not," I asked, " if they were only real French ? "

. " Yes ; but Cousin Annie says that they are not French, and I think they are not."

I was not at all obliged to Cousin Annie for interesting herself in the matter, but as she was n't under my control, I was obliged to counteract her influence in the best way I could.

It was less trouble to convince her that the flowers were French than to change them. Indeed I could n't change them for the better. I had nothing wherewith to do it. I did n't know whether the flowers were imported or not ; I bought them for French flowers, and I intended ·to sell them for French flowers.

I went to a box where a number of old labels had been thrown, — I am obliged to keep such a receptacle for the benefit of a certain class of customers, — and took out one printed with blue ink in French. Whether it was printed in New York, where I bought the flowers, or in France, goodness only knows, I don't. The facilities for making French flowers, and printing French labels in New York are great. It would be no far-fetched conclusion to infer that those were done there. I am under no obligation to tell my customers my suppositions.

I took the label to the glue-bottle, wetted the end of it, and fastened it around the stem of the bunch of flowers from which hers were taken. I kept her entertained with a new Paris fashion-plate till the glue was dry. Then I showed the flowers, compared them with hers, and exhibited the French label attached. Her skepticism was vanquished. She was convinced by such proof that her flowers were of no doubtful origin.

She departed hugging to herself the comforting assurance that she wore " real French flowers." My risibles remained in a quiescent state in view of her vanity, and my own effrontery. Nor does my conscience reproach me in revision of my act. Perhaps it has passed through the searing process necessary to destroy sensibility. It is certainly able to endure a very high temperature at present.

In examining the matter closely, I really think I performed a virtuous and amiable act in humbugging the little thing. She was in depths of trouble, and very miserable when she came in the 'store. I relieved her mind of its burden, and sent her on her way rejoicing. I congratulate myself that this day's low-descending sun has seen from my hand one worthy action done.

Still, in charging my accounts of right and wrong, I hardly know on which page to make the entry. I think it must be on the right. I had no other flowers wherewith to satisfy the child, and the label did.

VIII.

" You are a Christian ! " said Gracie to me to-day after I had borne a two hours haggling over the price of a bonnet, and received a great many impertinent remarks the while.

" Why so ? " not that I did n't take her meaning; but I liked to hear what she thought of the exhibition we two duals had furnished her.

" To stand there and let that woman try to injure you in that way, without saying a word ! " she replied in great indignation.

" Did you think she meant to injure me ? "

" Certainly ! what else could she mean ? "

" I think she meant to get her bonnet cheaper than I offered it. She had no wish to injure me. She forgot that I was any thing but an automaton bonnet-seller, out of whom it was incumbent ·upon her, in doing her duty to herself, to make the best bargain that she could. She was so self-engrossed that she never thought of my feelings or interests at all."

" If I had been in your place I would have let her know with whom she was dealing; how saucy she was ! "

" Her manner was low-bred, and disagreeable. She was evidently ignorant of any other way to behave, and I did my best, by my example, to teach her better."

" Teach her better ! " my little woman exclaimed, as though the very idea were preposterous.

" Well, Gracie, if I could n't teach her better by keeping my temper, I certainly could n't by losing it, and that would be strictly my own loss."

It is a popular saying that sins of ignorance God winks at. I don't know how that may be ; but if I am literally to follow such an example, I might as well send my eyelids, at once, to the Patent Office to secure the right of perpetual motion.

Taking it for granted that I am to be kept in a state of perpetual winking, my eyes must necessarily find intermediate space between the opening and shutting of the lids wherein to make observations, and draw inferences.

It cannot be fairly assumed that winks are blindness. though many are disposed so to construe them, and behave as though the Almighty, and all of His creatures were blindfolded, which is not the kind of wink under consideration.

Winks, like all other human actions, may be inferred to possess character which will admit of being resolved into classes.

A charitable wink at the faults of others might be construed, by the faulty, into ignorance or blindness, and unless one is wary he may be taken advantage of. An educated ignorance or blindness may be useful knowledge to a store-keeper, without one jot of principle in its exercise. A proper, discretionary use of policy, to give it useful direction, is all that is necessary. It would be entirely superfluous to inform the winked-at of his mistake, if he supposed the shop-keeper blind.

The greatest ignorance, the most profound unwisdom, in the aforesaid public and prominent person of store-keeper, would be to allow his winks of ridicule, contempt, or resentment, to make an egotistic display of their aptitude in the way of observation.

A large part of the impertinence which customers display is chargeable to that distinguished, but irresponsible character denominated Education.

The first lesson which a child is taught in shopping is, to get as much candy as possible for his penny. He is taught to pick over a basket of oranges, and to select the largest and fairest for his penny. If the candy is broken or the orange has a speck of decay in it, the shop-keeper is berated for a cheat. On that model the shopping manners of the child are formed.

Well, let the wink of charity cover that woman's ignorance, because the sore of vexation has not arrived at suppuration.

MAY 15, 18—.

To get fine dress has been said, by some uncharitable reformer of the male gender, to be the chief end of woman. How much precious time has been spent by that benevolent class of persons for the reform of the gentler sex. It is really astonishing what an amount of gratuitous effort has been put forth in its behalf.

It is to be desperately feared where so much has been attempted abroad that homesteads have been neglected. Indeed, we have actually seen unsightly weeds and thorns growing in the same soil with the tree of knowledge, — *i. e.*, knowledge of woman's short-comings. Rack and ruin have actually come before the face and eyes of the female pupil, upon her transcendent reformer's native paradise, and so blind was he to the state of things at home that the weeds and thorns had shaped themselves into the tree of life before his imagination.

" To be wise in our own eyes, to be wise in the eyes of the world, and to be wise in the eyes of our Creator, are three things so very different as rarely to coincide," was one of the old saws in vogue in my childhood.

Generous manhood ! to compass its own downfall in favor of woman's salvation ! But keen as man's penetration into woman's faults has been, other re-connoitering has been more thorough. My field of observation has been carried farther still into the enemy's quarters, and spied out a stronghold of sin which man has never discovered, or, at least, never spoken of. Probably the reason of the obliquity of his vision in this direction, was owing to inner blindness, the disease that originates within the purse.

The reformers, having pertinent reasons for leaving their own mental blindness unmedicated, those same reasons have operated to avoid making attack on woman's foible in the quarter referred to, and also have been the occasion of overlooking the occupation of the stronghold. But in order to victory all strongholds must be taken. If ever woman is redeemed, she must be cleansed from all sin. I therefore respectfully recommend to all generals commanding, that this point of fortification in wrong-doing be immediately besieged. I would recommend that all the guns in the reforming service, of all grades, be immediately brought to bear upon it; all, from the thundering cannon to the little lead pop-gun, in one grand trial of military skill, and see if it can be reduced to submission.

We allow, for the sake of appearing amiable, that the chief end of woman is to get fine dress, and that the chief end is reprehensible. Now I wish to have conceded, not on the score of amiability, but of truth, because I wish to have my statement based upon a sure foundation, that she has a chiefer end, and that chiefer end is to get fine dress cheap.

The chief obstacle in obtaining this concession from male reformers will be blindness to the fault which disease of blindness originates, as I have before stated, in the purse. As their purses usually furnish the means by which woman obtains fine dress the strings will, in the involuntary contraction which is a development of the disease, be drawn tightly over the pupils of the eye, so as to exclude the view of the fault. The disease runs higher than blindness. Like most of the devices of Satan to blind men's minds, this fault assumes the form of a virtue, and robed in the beautiful garment of economy stands out before men's eyes in commanding admiration. And it is admired, and praised, and flattered, and rolled upon the tongue as a very sweet morsel.

Undoubtedly one reason of the different view which male reformers take of the chiefer end of woman from what I do, is the different way in which we stand affected by it. I must adhere to my original opinion as to the chiefer end, and its chiefer reprehensibility, because that fault interferes more with my interests than the fault of the chief end. It appeals also more forcibly to my philanthropy. I see that the indulgence of it involves the destruction of woman's honesty, while the former sin only comprise, the deifying of her vanity, which comes under the lesser head of idolatry.

Time will prove whether male reformers will concede my point or not, but it is fairly to be supposed that they will not. Because a man convinced against his will is of the same opinion still, and he wills to remain blind, for the reason that his blindness saves him the trouble and expense of correcting woman's chiefer fault, — which reformation it lies in his power to correct by furnishing sufficient means to obviate the necessity of her practising such arts as she does to accomplish her chiefer end.

IX.

THAT doctrine of total depravity, which bore with such weight upon the theological discussions of reverend divines in my younger days, — it has lost its prestige in later years, — was always a stumbling-block in the way of my belief.

I was always a little skeptical about its orthodoxy, owing to the overflowing affection with which youth is endowed for all human things. I have been led to reconsider my juvenile speculations, in the light of maturity, or, in other words, in the character of womankind as presented to me through the glass of business, and I find that the doctrine assumes greater plausibility.

The change has n't been wrought by any special work of grace in my heart. My convictions have come altogether through the agency of my senses, the organs of sight and hearing. To define. These agencies having been employed in making observations, while I was engaged in selling bonnets, upon the human instrumentalities that bought them.

I am not putting down descriptions of these samples of total depravity, in order to compare the different degrees manifested by the different persons;

but to note the variety of talent put forth by each
to compass its object. I am a great admirer of
talent, hence my disposition to analyze, understand,
and preserve a record of its capabilities.

Really the difference in the quality of sins committed by depraved humanity, rests chiefly in the
different tastes of those who commit them. It seems
to me that in woman the total depravity crops out
more luxuriantly in the exercise of shopping than
in any other way. The opinion may be attrib-
utable to the point of vision from which I view it,
and the atmosphere through which I look.

Self-interest is not a good telescope, its opera-
tions being directed to objects too far off; but the
microscope is an exceedingly useful instrument, it is
so easily applied to objects at hand. I have no particular motive in examining the morals of those with
whom I have nothing to do, unless it is in a general
way when I give a dissertation on the sins of com-
munities. Then, it is very convenient to make a
packhorse of some remote region, but it is very desirable to see those with whom I deal every day
manifest a high moral standard.

To-day brought me one of the oily type of depraved humanity, to see how cheap she could get
a bonnet done over.

The first thing she told me was how cheaply she
could get it done elsewhere; she spoke with a voice
sweet and soft as a rippling rivulet. That is a favorite method to cheapen goods, a nice little birch

argument to hold over the head of a tradeswoman.
The very first stroke set my nerves ajar. If any
one thing more than another will arouse my human
nature it is a threat. It was an old bonnet, and
would make us more trouble to do than we should
get pay for ;· but I would n't have minded that if she
had shown any mercy in using her rod.

She had improvised herself into a penny-post to
report the affairs of my neighbors. Was it for my
benefit, or her own ? I could n't take oath upon
that point, because no court will allow a witness to
swear as to other people's thoughts, but I should be
perfectly willing to affirm as to my opinion. Her
despatches were not official, and I did n't feel disposed to pay for them, especially as they contained
matter of no importance to me.

I told her pointedly that I had nothing to do with
regulating prices in other stores; but I must certainly be judge of them in my own.

"I like your styles," she said, smooth as oil, determined not to be bluffed ; "but I really can't
afford to pay your prices."

I made no farther reply, but waited what I
thought a reasonable time for her to come to a conclusion ; but she stepped about looking over the
shop. At every step she took her boots gave out a
little creak that made me shiver all over. I found
there was no such thing as finishing her up in the
ordinary way. I must take her on some original
tack if I were to get rid of her without putting

down my price. She was determined to have my
styles, and equally determined not to pay for them.
I was obliged to resort to stratagem to bring matters to a head.

Query : If stratagems are allowable in love and
war, why not in trade ?

I looked her all over with a decided stare, so that
she might notice that I was examining her dress.
Then I threw as strong an expression of pity into
my countenance as I could command, and modulat-
ing my voice to a low tone, said, —

" I think, from your manner of talking, you must
be poor. If that is the case you need n't be afraid
to tell me, and I will consider you. As we are
strangers I don't know how you are situated ; but in
my poorest days I never turned my back upon the
needy. If you have n't the means to make yourself
tidy for church, I will do your bonnet for cost; or
will give you the whole, if it will distress you to pay
for it."

She tried hard to interrupt me ; but I went rapidly forward to propound my benevolent intentions.

" Oh don't thank me ! indeed, I don't deserve
thanks ! I am only fulfilling the command to help
those that need help, and to be kind. I always feel
richer after I have helped some poor woman to get
a living. I feel as though I had deposited in a safe
bank when I 've given to the poor. I feel as though
I had laid up something to fall back upon if I should
be poor and needy myself."

6

I was obliged to pause here to restore equilibrium to my lungs.   She broke in upon the silence, which my necessity enjoined, with a vehement disclaimer,—

" I am not an object of charity ! "

I had a very strong suspicion at the commencement of my address that she was not. I did'n't know her name, but I had seen her in church in the same slip for several consecutive Sabbaths. She had sat beside a well-dressed, middle-aged man whom I took to be her husband. Both had a well-to-do air, and bore unmistakable signs of having a competence.

" Beg your pardon, ma'am, if I mistook the bearing of your remarks," I went on meekly. Then I turned my tone to one of anxiety: " I really begin to have serious apprehensions that this whole community are becoming paupers. Can you inform me if that is so ? "

"Paupers ! what do you mean ? " she asked, in apparent terror at the supposititious calamity that was spreading itself over her beloved city.

"There used to be abundance, more than that, wealth in this city. Now I hear but one continuous cry of poverty. I was wondering what kind of accommodations could be provided if the whole community should be thrown upon the city authorities for support."

" I am no pauper ! " she indignantly exclaimed, " and never expect to be ! "

" I am glad to hear that assertion ; " I answered gravely. " My mind is relieved of one anxiety. Now

we will see what your bonnet needs in order to make
it becoming in the present era of fashion, to you,
and to your independent station in life."

"It is true we are in independent circumstances,
but I think it is a duty to be economical," she said;
a little doubtful of my meaning, but perfectly collected as to her own purposes.

She was determined to stick to me like warm
sealing-wax, till she accomplished her purpose; I
thought I might as well make entertainment for the
inner dual, — I could turn her to little account for
the outer, — so I went on to ask, —

"What is your idea of economy? There are so
many definitions of the word that one gets confused
as to the meaning of it, in applying it to his own
use."

"Economy!" she exclaimed in astonishment at
my ignorance. "I should think any simpleton
might understand that! How are you going to get
along in trade if you don't practice economy!"

"I have my own ideas of the virtue, and its application to every-day life. I asked yours, thinking I
might learn something new about it."   •

Don't impute naughtiness to me in this under-
hand thrust. It is sufficient punishment and morti-
fication to be convicted of malice by my own conscience when I was laying the flattering unction to
my soul, that I was drawing out her ideas, in order
to enlighten her ignorance, and elevate her morals
to broader views and practice.

" It is very easy to define economy," she answered
in good faith, " it is to save all you can, and make
every thing go as far as you can."

" In every direction, out of every one with whom
you have to do, and save it for yourself?" I asked.

" Certainly! I guess you understand it, all milliners do.   They get their work done for nothing, and
then charge an awful price for it."

I looked up to see Gracie's eyes snap and her
lips part.   That restored me to self-possession before
I spoke.   I smiled at the girl's red face, which manifested the workings of the inner dual, and went on
quietly to answer my customer's last remark.

" I can answer for only one milliner; I pay my
girls the highest wages that any can command.   I
don't leave it there, I see to it that it is enough to
feed and lodge them well, and then that there is re-
mainder left to clothe them comfortably."

" I suppose you work them early and late to make
up for your care; that's the way other milliners do."

" If they are well fed they are bright and active
through the whole season.   That is one of my ideas
of economy; and they can't get good board unless
they get wages enough to pay for it.   If other milliners oppress the hireling in his wages, I am not
responsible for it.   As to working early and late, I
never allow them here over ten hours, and I presume if you keep a servant, that you get fourteen
at least, out of her, and get her just as cheap as you
can."

"I pay my girls as much as I can afford to. If they don't like the wages I pay they can go where they can get more." She ignited at once at my remark; but I was expected to hear meekly, without reply, revilings which I had brought on my head by belonging to a craft. Well, well! Poor dog Tray suffered for the company he kept. "I know best what I can afford to pay. And I mean to keep 'em busy, to keep 'em out of mischief, if nothing else."

"That is all I claim to be allowed to do, to regulate the affairs in my own domain, set my own prices, pay my girls what I think best, and work them as hard as I please."

"My goodness! if you don't work them but eight or ten hours you'll certainly fail." She was getting deeply interested in my affairs. "I had two milliners board with me over two years, and they never got home, in the busy time, Saturday nights, till after twelve o'clock."

"My economy does n't operate in that way; I am such a stupid thing that I get tired and sleepy after ten hours of diligent work, and what I can accomplish after that is of little worth. If I rob myself of rest to do that little, my fatigue extends to the next day, and I can't accomplish more than half as much as I would to have left off the night before in proper season, and taken my rest. I judge my girls by myself. You see what poor economy it would be for me to overwork them."

"People do stand it to work so all their days, and make money by it."

"Yes, ma'am; but it depends something upon the kind of work that is done, and something upon the constitution of the person working, how many those days will prove to be, if twenty hours out of twenty-four are devoted to hard work. If he is exercising in the open air, the same individual will bear a much greater strain upon his health than if he were sitting in-doors, working in a confined atmosphere. You must have observed that most indoor hard-workers break down at, or before, middle life. Another consideration to be taken into the account is, who one is working for; it requires double the outlay of strength to do the same work for another, that it does for one's self. I know just how I want my own work done, and all I have to do is to execute it according to the idea formed, and that is distinctly before my mind. In doing for another, I must exert myself to understand his idea, then the care to execute it according to the imperfect conception which I must necessarily form of the model of another, is greater in the fear that I may not execute it according to his design. The increase of care produces increase of fatigue, or exhaustion of vital energy."

She did n't seem at all to comprehend what I was saying; my economy took so entirely different a range from the beaten track in which her own had always travelled. She thought she must say something more in defense of her position. Her reply was characteristic.

" I think if girls can play they can work, and if you don't keep them at work they are running the streets, and getting into mischief. For my part, I think it is best to keep girls at work till they are tired enough to go to bed."

" As to running the streets, that is the very best thing my girls can do after sitting all day bent over their work. By all means let them straighten themselves and run! It does n't follow at all that they must get into mischief. Good girls will be good everywhere, and bad ones will be bad anywhere."

Still she kept step-stepping, and her boots creak-creaking. I was half distracted; and in my desperation I resolved, if her selfishness had a salient point, to touch it on the quick. I took up the axe, and gave another blow with all of my might at what I thought was the root of the tree. I spattered a little cant on my hands, so that the handle would n't slip and glance from the telling direction. Then I went to work, and dealt blow upon blow, till the perspiration oozed from my face in running streams.

" I consider the effort to get all one can out of every other person, without regard to what is given in return, just stealing in order to gratify covetousness; breaking two commandments at once. If I do your work for little or nothing, or economically, as you call it, I must pay my girls economically and work them hard. I have no disposition to become like the task-masters of Egypt; nor will I do it if I starve. Neither am I willing to come under such a task-master as you. If you are willing to pay me a fair price, so that I can live honestly and honorably among my fellows, I should like to do your work, and will do it to the best of my ability. But if you are determined to live all you can out of me, and, in consequence, compel me to live as little as possible myself, I prefer that you should go somewhere else. I presume you will find plenty of your own moral calibre to deal with. Now you understand me."

"I hope you are not offended," she said apologetically, in her liquid tone. I suppose she thought herself the very personification of Christian charity and forbearance. "A soft answer turneth away wrath." Her words were soft as melted butter, but sharp as a razor. My righteous indignation was not to be so appeased.

"No, ma'am, I'm not offended, but I'd like to have you decide about your bonnet, as my time is my money, and I must be saving of it."

"I will leave the bonnet. You look honest, and such outspoken folks generally are. But you'll do it as cheap as you can, won't you?" she turned and asked when she had creaked half the length of the store toward the door.

I gave her a parting smile as I said, "Yes, ma'am." The smile was not one of approbation; it was called up by her display of the ruling passion in her last injunction.

X.

THE girls were having a great frolic when I came in this morning, over a little, mean, pinched-up looking bonnet which they had found lying on the table. Each was accusing the others of taking it in, and denying the doing it herself. They were so much engaged in their fun as not to see me till I stood in the midst of them. When they saw me they displayed its comicalities, and asked me where it came from. A little shiver of discomfort went all over me. I did n't reprove them, because they knew nothing of the history of the bonnet, and I knew the whole of it.

I replied very quietly that, " I took it."

" But we can't do any thing with it," they all exclaimed in a breath. " It is so rotten it won't hold together to do over, and there is n't any thing of it."

" Wait awhile, girls, till I tell you the story of that bonnet." I put away my own, and sat down. " Two days ago a poorly but tidily dressed girl came in, and stood shyly at the lower end of the shop. I thought she was afraid to come up, and was watching a chance to speak to me; so I went toward her, and asked if she wanted any thing."

" She looked up timidly, but still held back what she had in her hand. ' I 'm afraid,' she said, ' to show you my bonnet, — I 'm afraid you 'll laugh at it, and I 'm afraid it can't be done over.'

" I drew her a little one side, and told her not to be afraid ; I would n't laugh at it.

" You ought to have seen her watch me when I took it. Her look was as eager as though life and death hung upon what I said about it.

" I asked her, if that was all the bonnet she had ; and she said, ' Yes.'

" I asked, ' Can't you earn money to buy a better one ? '

" She said, ' Yes, but I can't spare it.'

" I asked, ' Why ? '

" She replied ' I have to support the whole of them now ; mother is sick, and can't help me at all.' Then she added in a tone of disappointment, ' I meant to have me a real pretty bonnet this spring, and I could if mother had n't been taken sick. But this one must do now, I can't possibly get another. I don't want to stay away from meeting and Sunday-school.'

" I asked her what she did, and where she worked ; and I 've been down this morning to see if she told the truth. Her employer gave her an excellent character, and said she was very industrious, — that she had been working extra hours for two months."

" I 'm sorry I made fun of the bonnet," said

Gracie with tears in her eyes. " I thought it belonged to some stingy old Putty-mutty-fudge-poor, like that India-rubber woman that was in yesterday."

" I called the girl out. She was pale with terror when she saw me. ' O don't tell me you can't do any thing with my bonnet,' she exclaimed.

" I told her I thought we could fit up her bonnet, and that I came to ask where her mother lived, so that I could go and see her.

" She told me ; but added, ' I don't think she can do any work for you, she is too sick.'

" I went directly where the mother was, and found her looking very ill. There were two little girls, too young to go away to work, that had to be taken care of, beside the mother. Now, girls, what shall we do with the bonnet ? "

" Perhaps I can find one that will do better than that," said Gracie. And she brought forward one or two that were a little damaged. " We girls will pay for one of these among us."

" You may fit up one of those. Trim it up from the piece-box. You can do it after your work-hours are over. You might do it in work-hours, only it won't be half so pleasant to do it all at my expense, as it will to make a little sacrifice yourselves."

" What can we do about her working extra hours ? " asked Gracie.

" We will all help a little, and take off one hour a day at least," they all answered.

" Why did n't you give her employer a lecture on oppressing the hireling in his wages, and grinding the face of the poor, as you did Putty-mutty-fudge-poor yesterday ? " asked Gracie.

" Her employer happened to be that notable woman's husband. At least, he is the man I 've seen at church with her. Probably he is like her in his ideas of economy, and all that it would have been proper for me to have said under the circumstances would have been said in vain. I was on the defensive yesterday. It would hardly be good policy to deal so plainly in an attack on one's own ground.

" If I am not in when she comes for her bonnet Saturday night, ask her who her Sabbath-school teacher is ; then we can put them all in a way to be taken care of. Blessings on the systematic charity practiced by churches."

So far I went with the girls ; but the inner dual went on, and on, in its wonderings. Why is it that churches do so much for the poor, when many of their members are so shockingly avaricious in their private conduct ?

Is it man's pride turned by the Disposer of all events to good account? Many a fund has been sunk by united effort for the benefit of the suffering when single effort would, for the same end, have remained inactive. Charity says it is done by the element of kindly sympathy which runs from heart to heart and stimulates to good from associating together. Cynicism says it is spiritual pride vaunting itself. Many a man who will compel his wood-sawyer to take his pay in sour molasses Saturday night, will swing the bank-note he made by the economical operation around his head the next day in the presence of the great congregation, and place it on the offertory. Many a man, who, when he thinks no one knows it, will let a poor girl work extra hours, because he will not pay enough for regular work to enable her to live comfortably, till she is reduced to a skeleton, will, when in the presence of his brethren, subject to their scrutiny, wax eloquent in pleading her cause by word and deed.

Many a man will let his neighbor lack for bread because he does n't belong to the same church he does. The same man will send a round sum to the benighted heathen, if his name may but soar up in heavenly altitudes, kite-like, before the public. with a long list of figures trailing out behind it, on a news-paper breeze of applause.

"Judge not that ye be not judged." A man can-not settle his brother's account with his Maker; but he can be diligent in all seasons to let his own works praise him, by making offerings with the right hand which the left hand knoweth not of.

MAY 22, 18 —.

That sweet, refreshing Rosie May came in this morning. Quiet, simple child! Strange she has n't made up a style of airs and manners for herself! She must be nineteen. Perhaps, wicked thought, she has arrived at a finished education, and taken her diploma in the graduating tactics of artificial manners and fanciful deportment, skilled in the art of concealing art. And perhaps she is one of those sweet-tempered anomolies that Nature occasionally throws in among her standard productions, to show what life might be, and what we hope to find it in the other land.

Sweet spoken, but prompt, and direct to the point as a man of business, she said : —

" I came in for you to fit me to a travelling head-gear just now. I wish to select a low-priced, white straw. I think a Pedal braid will do ; I shall probably be obliged to trouble you to take out a few strands, as ma thinks my face too long and narrow for the present style. A plain green ribbon, ma thinks, to trim it with, not very expensive ; but I like a green and white check, I think it looks younger. Now, if you please, I will look at what you have that you think best adapted to my purpose ; and we will decide between us. I have never selected a bonnet without ma's advice, but she sent me to you, and told me to say, if you could help my choice, and it suited all round, — you must know that includes papa as well as herself, — she would trust us to get up my dress bonnet. Then, all the trouble she would have would be to order her own. And as she is n't very well, I like to save her all the care I can."

I took at once. The bonnet was to be simple, suitable, in good taste, and when it was sent home the bill must suit papa. I know Judge May's family by report, and report usually gives the true version of character, although idiosyncrasies are almost always exaggerated by the public voice. I had no fear in suiting the Judge. His heart's blood would have been poured out freely to adorn that beautiful child. I had heard that Mrs. May was a little particular.

"I will try to suit you all," I replied, as I went to fetch a bonnet or two.

"So Mrs. Tallmadge told ma, and she told her it would be perfectly safe for me to come alone. You won't think I am impertinent, or trying to flatter you by telling what she said; but I do think it is pleasant to know when we please people." The amiable little thing understood how to do her part well. To make happy in view of my power to please was to give me courage and confidence in myself to make farther attempts. It was also to secure my best efforts in her service.

Be that as it may, it was her confidence, her belief in me that captivated me. There was no temptation to make a good trade. If there had been, policy would have defeated it. The Mays would be quick enough to find me out; and then, in the end, I should lose more than I should gain.

I looked out a couple of nice-looking Pedal braids and brought them to her.

"I think these are about the size for you, and about the quality you were looking for. They may look a little high at the top now, but as the form has just come in they will probably be made higher. I think I would n't have my bonnet lowered. When you become familiar with the sight of them they won't look so high."

"Of course they won't! we did n't think of that. Ma does n't like extremes in fashions; neither does she like me to look old-fashioned; and if it were too low it would look old-fashioned before the season was over."

I tried one of the bonnets on her head, and asked her what she thought.

"It looks monstrous to me; but I can't really tell any thing about a bonnet till it is trimmed. If you think it will do, trim it. Only if ma thinks it is too high it will have to come down."

"If, after wearing it and seeing others, you think it is too high I will change it."

"The thing is, not to look behind the times, or in the extreme of fashion so long as I wear it. You can judge best about that. I don't wish to think any thing more about it after it is done."

I showed her plain green ribbons, and checks. She asked the prices; and then selected what she thought would do.

"What kind of a flower shall I put in the face?" I asked.

"Dark rose-color, and not much of it. I shall be plainly dressed when I wear that bonnet."

I showed her some flowers. She made her selection, saying: "If you think that will do."

"Shall I put in joint-blonde or illusion?" I asked.

"You may put in whichever costs the least."

Her order was finished.

When the bonnet is sent home, it will be examined and decided upon. The bill will be looked over. If it suits, I shall be told so, and the bill will be paid. If it don't suit, it will be sent back, and just the change required will be pointed out. If all my customers were like that, I could open a "cheap store." I could do double the amount of business that I now do in the same time, and that would allow me to do it cheaper. Getting more profits in number, I should require less in amount, to make a living.

If Mrs. Tallmage were like the Mays, I should feel conscience-stricken for the trick I had put upon her, now that she has formed so good an opinion of me, and taken pains to circulate it in my behalf.

Nonsense! If she were like the Mays there would be no occasion for me to resort to stratagem with her, in order to get my dues. May-be in spreading me she had the displaying of her own shrewdness much more at heart. If she has discovered that the new store deserves patronage, and has so witnessed for me, I'll endeavor not to cheat her in that indorsement. I am extremely obliged to her for sending me such customers as the Mays.

What encouragement such patronage infuses into

7

business! Tallmadge has redeemed herself through her friends. I shall hereafter pronounce her a good customer, manifesting her goodness in the way peculiar to herself. Let her follow the bent of her own inclination in her efforts in my behalf, so long as she exerts herself effectually.

I will pronounce her an excellent woman to you, my Journal, and to the rest of my special friends. Not even in the work-room will I sputter a word to her disadvantage, or make a questioning shrug of the shoulders when she is mentioned, or an insinuating nod of the head. I will not make an offensive pen-mark. I will take back all I expressed to you in confidence the other day, my Diary.

Milliners are like other people. Put them in good humor with themselves, and they are in good humor with all the world.

XI.

YESTERDAY, just as I was at that interesting period of glorifying myself, and that other party with whom I am concerned, womankind in general, the Mays and Mrs. Tallmadge in particular, "Putty-mutty-fudge-poor," as Gracie christened her, made her appearance again.

My heart fainted within me! Adieu to the genialities of trade and the excellences of human nature therein displayed. She brought another lady with her, and I was justified, by my former experience, in supposing that they had brought another India-rubber stretcher whereon to induct my patience into the mysteries of the inquisition of trade.

"Putty-mutty-fudge-poor" said she just stepped in, — she might more fitly have said creaked in, her boots continued to give out their music, — at the time appointed, to see if her bonnet was done. It was no matter if it was n't. She was passing, and she thought she would drop in.

"Your bonnet is done, ma'am, and I hope it will suit you." I turned away to get it, and I heard her say in a loud whisper to the lady who was with her:

"Done it is the first time in my life that I ever

went for a bonnet, and found it done. I guess she is to be depended upon, but she 's awful independent, and you 'll have to do just as she says."

I saw that I had been discussed; in fact, I was going through the old lady's sieve. When I carried the bonnet to her she said, —

" You 've been very punctual ; " in a tone that implied, ' you 've been a good girl, and must be praised a little.'

" Is it any thing very remarkable for a woman to keep her word ? " I asked, and rather scornfully, I think upon reflection.

" Yes, it is ! " she replied emphatically. " I have always been obliged to carry my bonnet three weeks, certainly, before I wanted it; and I always went for it every day for three weeks after it was promised."

Poor dog Tray had to suffer again for being in bad company! I had no idea of taking another castigation for the misdemeanors of my crafts-women It is quite enough to suffer for my own sins, and I said rather tartly, —

" I think I have told you before that I don't consider myself responsible for what others do ; when you catch me tripping, tell me of it ! "

One story holds good till you hear another. I had no doubt but that she had worried and fretted other milliners in their prices, and crowded them down till they lost all interest in getting her work done. As it paid so little, it was put off till the last thing in the shop.

" Why did they treat *you* so?" I asked. I was bent on making her bear testimony against herself in favor of her milliners. I did n't doubt I should convict her out of her own mouth, when the whole story was told.

" Me! they treated me as well as they did anybody."

" That could n't be! everybody's work could n't be put off till the last."

" Everybody has favorites. I suppose the favorites got theirs done in season; but I consider my money as good as anybody's."

A great deal better, retorted the inner dual, or you would n't be so loath to part with it. What makes a customer a favorite with a milliner? I might have proposed, but I contented myself with saying, —

" Perhaps they can't afford, at the rates they are paid, to keep help enough to do their work in season."

" That was just so with the milliner that boarded with me. She did n't have but one or two girls in the shop the first of the week, only just enough to tend. Then, at the last of the week, she was hurried so she could n't get through the work she took. When my bonnet did come she brought it Saturday night with her, or rather Sunday morning. And you ought to see it, how it was done. The bows were pinned on, and the strings were wrong side out. One Sunday my whole top-trimming came off,

and I lost it on the street. And the border was all
flying out, like a flag of distress, on the wind."

" Why did n't she keep her girls all the week, so
as to have her work done properly ? " I asked ; but
the inner dual solved the question before her answer came.

She probably had to practice the same economy
that you do in consequence of having such customers as yourself.

" Because she did n't want to pay for only a half
week's work. She knew how to make her girls'
work tell."

Tell! echoed the inner, tell what ? that she robbed
her girls of half their time to save paying for it.
Did n't she really get as many hours' work from
them as though they were in the shop every day
in the week. Tell a tale of oppression ! Are not
you, and the like of you, one cause of the shameful
tale ? I contented myself with asking my impromptu
penny-post, sarcastically, —

" Did n't she do your work cheap ? "

The caustic question fell harmless.

" Oh yes ; I had no fault to find with her prices ;
but the work was done poorly. I used to have my
bonnet fixed two or three times before it would
stay together."

" The usual way of cheap work. If you had
paid her better she would have kept more help, and
your work would have been better done."

" No, it would n't. She wanted all the pay herself. She meant to get rich, and she has. She owns as much real estate as any man in the city."

I had no farther remarks to offer, but the inner dual exercised its office, and pronounced, Pretty equally matched with the people she deals with.

By this time she had looked her bonnet all over.

" Do you like it?" I asked.

" Yes, it looks better than I expected. Let me see the bill?" My hand trembled when I gave it her, in fear of an explosion. She looked it over, and her face lighted up like the sky after an April shower. My heart is a good reflector, pleasure flashed all over it.

" It is n't so much as I expected! I told him " — referring to her husband I suppose — " this noon when I asked him for the money to pay for it, that he need n't expect to get off with any such little bills as my bonnets had cost."

I drew a long breath of relief. My anticipated rating was not to be forthcoming. I am thankful for all favors received, and can be reconciled to those which are not bestowed, in the way of ratings, when they are withheld because a customer is satisfied.

" You had better try the bonnet, and see if it is all right."

"Try on a bonnet!" she exclaimed in astonishment. " Who ever heard of such a thing!"

" The face-trimming may need to be moved a little in or out," I answered.

"She does take pains to have every thing suit, don't she?" she remarked to her companion.

It was very evident to me why milliners had taken no pains to have her bonnets suit.

She then turned to me and introduced her friend: "This is Mrs. Miner. We fixed it up together that we were both coming here if you suited us; and I was going to try you on mine."

The tale was finished, the finale reached. I had stood the proof of their crucible, and come out the true metal. It had been a fiery trial to me, whatever enjoyment or benefit they might have reaped from it. If I had penetrated the dual woman at first, I doubt if I should have stood the refining as well.

Mrs. Miner proved very expeditious in transacting her affairs.

"All is well that ends well." In despite of my grumbling, " Putty-mutty" has ended well. I 'll make a pet of the first part of my unknown friend's improvised appellation, and make no mention of the latter syllables, " fudge-poor," so long as she behaves so admirably. But just so sure as she commences one of her economical antics, I shall put it on again as an indication of my disrespect.

The whole world has behaved beautifully to-day; and I retire to that state of repose which Sancho Panza has immortalized as the most blessed of inventions, prepared to enjoy its benign influence.

XII.

"THERE comes Mrs. Cheapside!" whispered
Gracie to me this morning, when she noticed a
certain lady coming toward the store. "You must
ask her more than you intend to take. She is
the terror of every dry-goods dealer in the city!
When I was tending at Mason's, one day I saw him
climb out of the back window and slide down the
water-conductor, to get rid of her. If I go to wait
upon her it will take the time of both of us. She
will send me to you to find out the least you will
take, if it is a yard of three-cent ribbon that she
wishes to buy. She was marked and sent round
long ago."

" 'Marked and sent round!' what does that mean
Gracie?"

"Every woman, and the way she trades, is known
in every store in town where she goes. One store-
keeper tells another, and all treat her alike. That
is what they call marking. If she is a good customer they treat her with attention. All want her
custom. If she is a poor one, they all get rid of her
the best way they can."

How mean Gracie's recommendation of asking
more than I meant to take looked to me. I was in

an amazingly upright mood just then. I was just tall enough to stand upright on my own dignity; or the stilts of integrity used by the one-price system. I would condescend to no such artifice to secure my customers, or my profits.

What different moods one finds one's self in at different times! I was not at all disposed toward the policy which seemed so desirable in the case of Mrs. Tallmadge. All of the arguments in favor of that policy were entirely out of my mind.

To mark a customer, and hand her round! Shocking! How low-bred tradespeople looked in my eyes! If such tattling was in vogue among them, I would keep myself from such society! The very thought was contamination.

> " Vice is a monster of so frightful mien,
>   That to be hated needs but to be seen."

And one better read in the workings of human nature than I am went on to say, "We loathe, then pity, then embrace." Now that I have looked at it all around, it seems to me a very good practice, that of marking and sending round to save time. If a customer is understood by one, the knowledge would be equally beneficial to the whole craft. Understood by all, and treated alike by all, the customer must see that she is in fault, and change her ways. Was ever human nature so convinced and made better? Perhaps not, but as new discoveries are being constantly made, in every direction, such an event may happen through the aid of some new invention in ethics. Cain knew that every man's hand was against him, and he must have more than suspected the reason why. If a woman is treated with disrespect in every store in which she goes to trade, she may have strong reason to suspect that she is not so treated on account of her good behavior. The only obstacle in the way of her coming to an understanding of the true state of things will be that, although she can see very distinctly the way in which others treat her, there is a natural impediment in her eye, called in the Book "a beam," which prevents her from taking cognizance of her manner of treating others.

Mrs. Cheapside asked to see bonnets. I showed them, and blandly explained the merits and beauties of each. They were all very pretty, but each one had some fault, especially the one she retained in her hand, — the one which I saw by the look in her eye she had made up her mind to have. She held the bonnet in her hand, but passed on to look at the flowers.

" Will those flowers be durable ? " she asked. " They look to me as though they would n't wear well. When I buy a thing and pay my money for it I like to have it last some ! "

" That is a well-made flower, and will last as long as any. The durability of flowers depends very much upon the usage they get. We buy flowers more for their beauty than their strength to endure hardship. Those are beautifully tinted, and nicely put together."

She took up a piece of ribbon that attracted her attention.

" Will that ribbon fade? " she asked. " It looks to me as though it would fade. I 've had milliners tell me a ribbon would n't fade, and then it did."

" All ribbons will fade in time, by exposure. Even black grows rusty, and white turns yellow. I think that as durable as any color."

" It is partly cotton, is n't it. It feels cottony."

" Perhaps so ! you don't wish to buy it." I was growing impatient, I was getting an insight into the marking and handing around arrangement, and its usefulness became apparent.

" If I conclude to take this bonnet, and get all my things here to trim it, you will throw in the work, won't you ? "

" No, ma'am ! " was my curt reply.

" You 'll take something off the price then ? "

" No, ma'am ! That is our price, and we consider it a fair one."

" I never patronize folks that don't take off any thing."

" Then I 'm afraid I 'll get little of your patronage."

" I like this bonnet pretty well."

I made no reply.

She went on : " We 've been building this summer, and I want to save all I can. I think you might take off fifty cents."

" That would be taking off more than my profit. I should be selling it for less than I paid."

" Well then, a quarter. As we 've been building, and it has cost so much, my husband will make a great ado about my bills. I must save all I can."

So far as she and her husband are concerned, I consider it their place to settle their own affairs. I could not, with any propriety, have any thing to do with them. I was on the point of explosion; but I made a mighty effort, and got the mastery of myself, if it did n't last long. I must say something, so I remarked, —

" It is every one's duty to save, and not to waste."

" Will you take off the quarter?" she persisted. " I must save all I can on my bonnet."

" Who do you wish to make your saving out of?" I asked. Little did the woman imagine with what utter disgust and repulsion I was looking at her unclothed spirit; or, rather, clothed upon with the deformity of its greed.

" Out of my bonnet, to be sure!" Was it possible that woman could be so blind as to what quarter her saving was to come from?

" There is one that will cost you less, then," I replied, and pointed to one lying on the table at a little distance off.

" Oh no!" she exclaimed in disdain; " I would n't wear such a bonnet as that! I want a good bonnet; but I sha'n't pay any such price as you ask!"

Sha'n't! echoed the inner. We 'll see about that. The time has come to be plain with you when you tell me what you shall or sha'n't do with my goods, and I said decidedly, —

"Then you can't have the bonnet. If you wish to save on your bonnet, as you represent, you must take a cheaper one. If you intend to save out of me, I, as a party concerned, protest against and resist the proceeding. If you take one of my bonnets you will take it at my price."

"This is the only bonnet in your store that I would wear; but I 've laid aside just so much for my bonnet, and I sha'n't pay any more."

"You must be your own judge of what you will pay for your bonnet, but you will pay my price for mine if you have it. The fact which you put forward, that you have been building, is no reason, in my view, for giving you a quarter in charity. It only shows, to me, that you have means in abundance to pay for what you want. And that you won't use it, only shows that you wish to filch your things out of others. If you wish for the bonnet at my price, you can take it. If you don't wish to pay that, the sooner you decide, and leave me to pursue my own business the better."

"You will get a great deal of custom by talking in that way," she answered angrily. "I will inform my friends what a reception I have met with."

I endeavored to prove myself her equal in sparring.

"If your friends would prove such customers as their acquaintance which you have introduced to me in your distinguished person, it would be quite a favor to keep them away. If they are not like you they will understand just how much of your report is reliable."

Query: Is it possible to maintain one's equinimity, or even to preserve an outside of civility to such customers? Ah! for the grace of patience spoken of at the commencement of this Diary, with courtesy appended.

Another query: Are there not a class of persons to whom Solomon's wisdom may be more appropriate in application than Job's. From the two equally reliable authorities, I have come to the conclusion that it is well to practice on the model of either as the merits of the case may, in my judgment, require.

She started in burning indignation to leave the store. When she reached the door, the cool air outside, or the still more cooling reflection that she was too well known to fare any better wherever she might go, allayed her heat, and she turned and looked at me.

I smiled. How she interpreted it I don't know; I was smiling at her predicament, — "marked and handed round." Was I mean enough to take advantage of that predicament to give her no quarter? Would I have treated one who bore a better name in the community, in the same way? The inner dual answered, Doubtless no! but as you will be sustained in it, you have done well, — she richly deserved it. *Vox populi vox Dei.*

She had come to me because I was a stranger, and just commencing business, — she could intimidate

me! She really cared nothing for what I said to her!
She had no sensibility! She cared nothing for what
I thought of her, provided she could accomplish her
object.

She came back, and took me on another tack.
Her one-sided hint about her husband now broached
itself in lachrymose complaint.

"My husband feels very poor now, he's spent so
much in building; he told me I must get my bonnet
with what he gave me or go without; and you know
what men are when they get cross. You can't do
any thing with them. I can't; mine is real hard on
me!"

I thought if her husband dealt any more plainly
with her, when he was cross, than I had, there must
be rather an uncomfortable state of things existing
between them. I said to her, without the slightest
scruple of delicacy, — I saw not the least occasion
to make covert suggestions; the plain, unvarnished
truth seemed to me in requisition, and I used it, —

"I have nothing to do with affairs that obtain
strictly between you and your husband, those are for
you to arrange between you." I thought if a little
advice came amiss, my mind would be at rest if I
vented it, so I continued: "I think the less a woman
says to strangers about her husband getting cross,
and denying her money, the more respectable both
parties will appear."

Finding me impervious to arguments, threats, and
entreaties, she gave in, and told me how she would
have the bonnet fitted up.

She then slunk out of the store, very much after the manner of those quadrupeds that snap and snarl in pugnacious grandiloquence till a smart rap on the nose tests their courage.

The power of love in restraining human passions, and renewing human hearts is infinite. But there is depth of wisdom contained in the method of instruction proposed by the wise man. The hand that holds the rod should be guided by discretion, and the motive-power that wields it should be love. Here love comes in again to the detriment of the rod. Whoever thought of chastisement when his heart was full of the joy of complacency? Let one get roused to indignation by wrong, or thwarted interests, or whatever may be the exciting cause, and the lashes, involuntarily, fall thick and fast on the offending culprit.

The rod that chastises with love may, safely, be supposed to be held in the hand of parental authority, or in the hand of the Great Father. Was the rod ever used in love by one human dual over another human dual occupying equality of position? May-be, but the record of such events, if made in truth, would be like the wells in the Arabian desert, long journeys apart.

There may be such an emotion as righteous indignation, it may be able to control itself so that no selfish resentment and retaliation be mixed up with its expression when it vents itself on the object which has aroused it.

8

XIII.

GRACIE came running into the back shop this afternoon, where I was superintending some work, with a most lugubrious expression on her face, and in tones that corresponded with the affliction depicted on her countenance, announced that she was waiting for Mrs. Bailey to decide.

"I wish you much happiness of your customer," was Sue's sympathetic rejoinder. "I have stood in her stretcher, waiting for her to decide, till in that tension my back was near leaving my company."

"I have stood three quarters of an hour by the clock," said Gracie; "and what do you think is the important question under consideration ?"

"Probably the shade of a pink !"

"It is whether she will wear a sprig of the lily of the valley, or ivy in her hair to-night."

"A question which it would have been very proper for her to have decided at home," I remarked.

"Decide at home !" echoed Sue. "She tried that when she was first married. Her husband, Ned Bailey, is my cousin. I've known her to keep him waiting for her to go down town with him after breakfast two long hours, deciding what dress she should wear. At first, out of politeness, he waited; but it made him so late to his business, and he lost so much by it, that he tells her now to go decide, and he'll come back for her to-morrow."

"That was what made you vanish so abruptly when you saw her coming," said Gracie ruefully.

"O Gracie, don't accuse me of unkindness. You know I would gladly lay down my life for you, provided the sacrifice could be accomplished by instantaneous decapitation. But to think of being sent out of existence by Mrs. Bailey's slow torture would be more of a sacrifice than my love for you could compass. Her inflictions may well be likened to dissolution under the death-blows of a lame spider."

"Shocking! shocking fatality!" was echoed through the room by various voices in a low whisper.

"She must have been subjected to Goodyear's process of vulcanizing, or she could never extend to such longevity of decision without breaking down. I have seen her seat herself at the counter at nine in the morning, and stretch herself out over the whole forenoon, till twelve, over a piece of No 1 ribbon to trim a dress. When the clock struck twelve she sprung up as bright, and bounded back as elastic as though she had never been drawn out at all. That was when she was the gum in its natural state, but now that she has been subjected to the improvements of matrimonial science there is no limit to her extendability. If she ever comes here to get a bonnet you will see her display the quality in all its glory."

Gracie clasped her hands and rolled up her eyes in an attitude of despair.

" May my good angels stir around in the air, and blow up a shower to wet Mrs. Tallmadge's new French bonnet all through, so that I may be employed in importing another when these glories shine forth."

And composing her countenance into an expression of patient resignation she retreated to attend to her India-rubber customer.

MAY 25, 18 —.

The rich and fashionable Mrs. Squire Stebbins has been in to-day. Her first statement was, that she wished to get a stylish and fashionable bonnet. The price was of no consequence.

That announcement was like cold water to a thirsty soul! It was good news from a far country! I was utterly overcome. It was a long time be-before I could realize that I was not the subject of an illusion. When I came fairly around, and had fully persuaded myself that I was really I, and that no illusion had run away with me, that it was I in my proper senses, I found sufficient stamina remaining in my nervous system to wait upon my customer in a collected and rational way.

The first thing I noticed was her eyes fixed upon me in a remarkable manner. She must have seen that something unusual had transpired. It was very evident that I was disturbed by some unexpected circumstances. With a jaunty toss of her head, and a little flutter all over, she remarked, spiritually, to the inner dual, You are surprised and confused to see so much elegance and fashion as I present to your bewildered gaze. It is to be hoped that you will soon get accustomed to the august presence, and its transcendent details, so that you can approach near enough to make your homage available.

The words still rung in my ears : She did n't care for the price! Was it an echo from Eldorado? What genii had transmigrated into the form before me to announce so astounding a communication? The woman must be in a spiritual trance ; if not entranced, she must be under the "influence," so as not to be cognizant of what was going on in the body. It was long before it became a fixed fact in my mind that she wished to get a pretty and becoming bonnet irrespective of cost. Even when that desirable point was arrived at, and settled in my mind, flashes of terror would strike all over me, at intervals, lest I was laboring under an illusion. The cold perspiration would start, in an agony of apprehension, lest she should disappear, and spirit away my visions of a golden opportunity wherein to display, unrestricted by the direful necessity to make something else do because it was cheaper, and so spoil it, my skill in millinery. If she did n't disappear altogether, might she not awake, and commence to haggle about prices?

It was full ten minutes before my stunned emotions gathered sufficient consciousness to ask, —

" What have you in your own mind ? "

" I have n't a single idea."

" Then I will see if I can start one.   What colors
do you wear ? "

" All at times.   I like a mixture.   Have n't you
bonnets made ? "

" Yes, step this way."

I knew I had nothing she would want ; but I must
keep her awhile, so as to study her.   If she proved
to have foreign tastes, in a day or two I could have
some bonnets in from New York of a new pattern,
and there must be one among them that would exactly suit her.   I showed her what I had.

" Have n't you some put away in your private
room ? " she asked.

That question opened her to me.   She was no
longer a sealed book ; I read her just as I would
read a printed page.   A New York bonnet she
must have, made by a French ' milliner at least.
And she should have it, regardless of cost, so far as
cost went to make up its beauty.

I saw too, from the question about the private
room, that Mrs. Tallmadge had been exercising her
vocation.   Glorious Mrs. Tallmadge ! may you be
blest in your basket and your store ! not in a milliner's store, but in having a full larder.   Is it possible
that she is acting upon the proverb " Misery loves
company ? "   Does she think she was entrapped to buy
an expensive bonnet, and her friends might as well
taste the same sweets ?   Or does she feel satisfied,

and wish to help me on in consequence? No matter, so long as I am benefited.

In about five minutes I had read Mrs. Squire Stebbins's complexion and features, and was prepared to make her a bonnet. If I were not a milliner I could n't help doing that. He that runs may read. She had printed her character all over her exterior. Both duals were stamped upon her dress and manners, and stood out to observation, like the staring gold capitals upon the black ground of the sign over my shop door.

But not to be limited in the expense I put upon the bonnet! That was the *summum bonum* of happiness in getting it up. As handsome a New York bonnet as I can extemporize she shall have. And she shall pay no more than the value of it. It must cost more than Mrs. Tallmadge's, or she won't be satisfied that it is so nice a bonnet. It must be a little better. She will judge of its value by the cost, that is her way. Unless she pays a large price an article is of no account with her. I must treat her accordingly. I have scruples about overcharging her, I hate to do it; but she must be satisfied, or she will never favor me again. Once gained, I should be sorry to lose her custom. She and Mrs. Tallmadge will compare bonnets, and tell the cost of each. I must tuck a little extra lace on Mrs. Stebbins's, to account for the difference in prices.

Dear, good soul! to leave me in the exercise of my free will! If she were predestinated to exercise

the doctrine of Arminianism toward me, she was
made the favored instrumentality of filling my cup
of millinery happiness to overflowing.   She shall
have her reward!   I will make her heart sing for
joy that her head sports the most expensive bonnet
to be found in the whole circle of her acquaintance.

I told her that I had none in, then, that she would
care for; but I was expecting patterns from New
York in a day or two, as soon as the next steamer
arrived, and that she should have the first sight of
and choice from them.

I was very careful not to say what kind of patterns.   I was expecting some new fashion-plates.
I announced the letter of the truth: who looks
deeper? or talks truer?

"They may be here the day after to-morrow; I
think I may safely count on them the day after that;
so that you may not be disappointed, put it off till
Thursday.   I shall certainly have them then."

"If they come the day before, you won't let any
one else see them?" she asked eagerly.

"Not an individual shall see them till you do."

"What time shall I come in?"

"About four in the afternoon!"

"That will be just the thing!   I'll come down
and walk up with the Squire to dinner, and take
him in with me to see the bonnets.   He is very fond
of seeing me handsomely dressed, and I like to gratify his taste.   If he don't like it, I sha'n't buy the
bonnet."

Admirable wife! as well as excellent customer! If you and your husband are not affinities your consummate management will soon make you so. You are endowed with an adroitness of wisdom for managing your husband worthy the imitation of your sex, — all of your sex that are married, and wish to live happily with the husbands of their choice, or of their convenience, as the case may be.

As soon as her back was turned, I began to execute my plans for making three bonnets. First, I collected what materials I had that I thought would do for them. Then, I turned every wholesale store in the city inside out to get just what I wanted, and every retail where they would oblige me. Was there any harm in spreading it around that I had some stylish orders to fill? I must take every pains to spread myself, so as to increase my trade.

And here let me announce to you, my Journal, for the credit of the craft, that in every retail store save one I was cordially favored. The one who refused me was my next-door neighbor. I did n't lay it up against her; but I hope I shall have an opportunity to oblige her some time. If I do, I 'll heap coals of neighborly kindness enough on her head to singe, if I cannot burn her hair off.

My next neighbor is very reticent in her way of doing business; report says, from fear that some of us vulgar milliners, who make bonnets for the common herd, should take advantage of her styles. She does millinery for a " set," and it is only following a law of Nature for her to imitate their manners, — *i. e.*

put on the same airs that they do. Of course milliners imitate their betters; why should n't they? The ways of superiors are always copied by inferiors. What do people set examples for if it is n't in the hope to have them copied?

In making a circle in which to include themselves and exclude others who are not favored with quite as much wealth, or what they call style, or what? — really I don't know what the requisites are for admission within the pale of Yankee aristocracy. If there is n't the obscurity of heraldry, there is the mystery of social free masonry about the indefinite, indefinable coat of arms which is quartered on some indefinite, undistinguishable shield, which it is necessary to inherit, or acquire, in order to be eligible to admission to some set. And the set just as mysteriously sets itself up as an example for imitation or admiration, so far as its superiority is apparent to any but the initiated. The merits of the case are beyond my understanding; but it is a wonderful common phrase that such and such an one belongs to one of the first families. I hear it every day in the shop. I have been led to infer that the phrase means, one of the families that first settled in the town. It is spoken of as a distinction to belong to one of the first families. If it confers distinction upon one's descendants to have settled first in a place, we must all obtain the distinction of belonging to the first families through our common parent, who took up the wild lands of the earth and settled them.

Perhaps some light may be thrown upon the sub-

ject by repeating some remarks made in my hearing
the other day. A lady said to another, on hearing it
said of a third that she belonged to one of the first
families, —

"I would n't care to have my great-great-grandfather's insignia of employment quartered upon my
patent, although he earned the money by it that
laid the foundation for wealth in our family. He
sold rum and molasses; not a chivalrous employment; but he made his family very comfortable by
it, and his descendants also. But I should hardly
consider it desirable to have a rum-barrel, tumblers,
and decanters, painted upon my pannels."

"I am in the same predicament!" echoed the
friend that was with her, " and everybody knows it.
And every new acquaintance I make will be sure to
look it up. My great-great-grandfather started the
wealth in our family by catching, and curing, and
selling fish. I must carry the odor of that fish around
with me as long as I live, and my children will
always smell fishy; but I don't think it would make
a very picturesque appearance upon my coach-door,
delightful as it may be to some of my disadmirers to
fish up the facts of my descent."

Those people who pride themselves on belonging
to the first families live in glass houses.

I am willing to let them abide in their social fol-
lies so long as they bestow substantial marks of favor
upon me by buying bonnets.

I have often thought I would like to know if they
really do think that they, and their things, are better

and look better than other people and other people's things.   If they do, they must be the class of people which the Book cautions against thinking more highly of themselves than they ought to think.   Excellent advice!

Why, oh why did Infinite Wisdom make us all of one flesh ?   When one was born to rule and another to serve, why could n't He have ordained a line of distinction by making the ruler of imperial blood to correspond with his upward tendencies, and the servant of base flesh and bones to comport with his lowly position?   What a world of contention such an arrangement would save in the great struggle which agitates mankind, and has agitated it since the world was in existence, the struggle of who shall be greatest!

Oh deplorable fact!   All people are made of one flesh, and of the same mental and moral elements, when the distinctions of rank, and distinctions of intellect, and distinctions of goodness are so desirable to promote the happiness of mankind! especially the happiness of those who are ambitious to be promoted.

Good-by, my Diary, my confidant.   I shall be too busy on my New York bonnets to tell you any more tales till day after to-morrow night.   I know it is good advice to " keep thy mouth from the wife of thy bosom ;" but you have no mouth, my Journal, and I have no wife of my bosom, therefore the advice cannot belong to me.

XIV.

THE wonderful event has transpired! The bustle and excitement of the celebration is over; the hour of calm reflection has come. In the light of retrospection I hope I may be able, truthfully, to record the successful honors with which the never-to-be-forgotten occasion has been crowned.

Precisely at the hour appointed the procession was formed. The music of the town-clock struck up, and Mrs. Stebbins swung the Squire into the store upon her right arm.

I marshalled them at once through the windings of the work-room into my sanctum, which was to be the theatre of exhibition. I seated my audience in two portly easy-chairs, in front of the stage, — the table, — and went on to make my exhibition, by my manner, as imposing as possible. I then held up before their delighted eyes the simplest bonnet of the three which I had made for the purpose.

My programme was to show the cheapest, plainest bonnet first, and keep the most showy, expensive one, the one I supposed she would buy, as the last great crowning show of the entertainment. I don't know why I did that; I think it was instinctive wisdom, or following of the habits of those who better understand managing human nature than I do.

I have often wondered why at theatres and other places of entertainment, the best performances are reserved till the last. It is very tiresome to wait through stupid scenes in expectation of them, but I suspect there is wisdom in the arrangement. The better the last scene the more pleasant will be the impression of the place after departure from it. The pleasanter the impression upon the memory, the more likely the person will be to return again to enjoy another entertainment. I certainly wished to make my customer so well pleased with the bonnet that she would buy it; not only that, but come again to buy another.

Mrs. Squire Stebbins went into beatitudes over the first bonnet I held up. No doubt she had prepared her ecstacies beforehand, and understood where to applaud.

She caught the bonnet from my hand, and exclaimed over and over again, —

" Is n't it a beauty, dear? Is n't it a perfect love?"

" Yes, Ducky, I 've no doubt it is," he replied, doing his best to sympathize with the emotions of his better half; " but you know I must see a bonnet on to judge how it looks."

She began to untie her own bonnet, in order to give the one she held in her hand the finishing effect of her handsome countenance. Some might call her a little too stout to be fine looking, and her face a little too full to be pretty. To me her fullness only betokened a bountiful table, and her placid countenance the repose of contentment produced by the quiet entailed in inheritance of a full purse.

The Squire was her counterpart, with an additional twinkle in his sharp black eyes, which would bear the interpretation of jolly.

I interrupted her purpose of putting on the bonnet, by telling her that I had one or two others that I would like to show her before she tried any.

She looked at them a few minutes in silence, and then gave vent to her delight, always addressing herself to the Squire.

"They are all loves, ain't they, Hubby dear? I really don't know which is the prettiest."

"They are all loves," echoed the Squire with a chuckle. "Put on one."

"I don't know which one to choose; I'm in love with them all."

"Don't make me jealous by giving me a rival in a bonnet; put on one, and swim round a little, Ducky, and let me see how you look."

"Which one, Hubby? I really don't know which is the prettiest, they are all so beautiful!"

"Either, no matter which; I can't tell any thing about a bonnet till I see it on."

I foresaw this dilemma at the commencement of the scene, and prepared for it. I saw that she was not able to choose her own bonnet, I must make the choice for her. She wished for a handsome, becom-

ing bonnet, and that was all she knew about it. She
wished me to understand her deficiency, and supply
it, but she would n't care to have her husband think
her a ninny; hence the little airs and graces put on
to cover up her ignorance.

She was keen enough in reading human nature, if
she could n't tell about bonnets, and adapting herself to those with whom she had to do.

When she came first to me she had Mrs. Tallmadge in her mind, although she didn't mention her.
She understood, and wished to put her own case in
opposition to that of the notable lady mayoress ; so
she told me to spare no expense.

I took up the one I had designed for her, and
said, — " This is the most expensive bonnet, but I
think it the handsomest and the most becoming one
for her."

" Put that on then," chuckled the Squire. " You
shall have the handsomest there is, so long as you
are Mrs. Squire Stebbins ; " and he tapped the floor
with his cane, and then put the shining gold head to
his lips.

Had it been a proper exhibition of satisfaction I
could have clapped my audience ; but as such dem-
onstrations usually come from the other side, I
maintained the dignity of my position. Such a sentiment was by no means vain or silly to my hearing,
but well worthy the stronger vessel who gave it utterance.

What mattered it that his vanity in Squire Stebbins, and his purse, and his position in the world, and all of his surroundings shone forth through Mrs. Squire Stebbins's new bonnet? His wife was a part of himself, a part of all these things, vanity included, and, most wonderful announcement of all, his wife was the sharer of his purse.

Squire Stebbins and Mrs. Squire Stebbins were one in the eye of the law, — they were one in the esteem of Squire Stebbins. Here was a glorious, compound, double duality! It was a feast of fat things, of wine on the lees well refined, without one drop of selfishness.

I forgot, for the moment, that I was selling a handsome bonnet at a handsome profit, in my joy to see that man reckon his wife bone of his bone and flesh of his flesh, a part of his outer and his inner life, the inner being that within the pocket.

Flesh she was, real, genuine adipose to an unknown weight, but making all due allowance for the enlargement which crinoline made to her borders, it might fairly be inferred to be a hundred and fifty pounds. If not given precedence as his "better half," she was duly indorsed as an equal part of himself. Not with lip acknowledgment, as many men theorize when they talk about their wives; but which theory subsides into subjection to interest when new bonnets and such like substantials are to be provided for her out of his substance.

His substance! echoes the inner dual. Why is it his substance? How do you maintain that propo-

9

sition? . How comes the financial substance of the
marriage partnership to belong to one party any
more than it does to one partner in any other partnership.   Both partners are equally interested,
spend equal time, and make equal efforts to maintain the establishment.   In every single instance?
No! nor are the labors and awards of every other
partnership adjusted to the perfect satisfaction of
every partner in every single instance.

A woman's time and labor are not worth as much
as a man's.   Let a man who thinks so take up his
time in doing what his wife does, and what he cannot get on without having done, and then he can understand how much time he would have left to attend to more important concerns.   It must be that
men jump to conclusions.

Squire and Mrs. Stebbins were affinities.   I luxu-
riated in that idea.   What are affinities?   This instance of affinities made the answer very plain.
Mrs. Squire Stebbins made it the one object of her
life to please Squire Stebbins, and Squire Stebbins
made it his first care in life to provide for the happiness and comfort of Mrs. Squire Stebbins.

The inner dual suggested, here is a simple and
natural solution of what has been considered by
some a mysterious, supernatural problem, — a problem which has been vainly attempting to explain itself for a long time through various matrimonial
heresies.   If Squire and Mrs. Stebbins are an example of affinities it is useless to go into spiritual

latitudes in order to make them. The example set by the uxorious couple need only to be followed by all married people, and the world will be full of affinities. And those affinities will stand out in bold relief, in grand and beautiful proportions, as large as life, against the shams and mockeries which now so frequently represent marriage.

The example of Squire and Mrs. Stebbins is like apples of gold in pictures of silver; but there would be no need to copy their manners, — manners are a matter of personal taste. It is necessary to practice only the spirit of the connection in order to insure success in an effort to secure affinities.

But take particular notice: if affinities are undertaken, in order to insure happy results, it is absolutely necessary that all who attempt to create them should individually follow the example of their prototypes. Unless this is done, the whole experiment will fail. The affinities will still continue to manifest themselves in the vague, unsatisfactory form hitherto represented, instead of the living, breathing, glorious realities exhibited by Squire and Mrs. Stebbins.

Only united effort can succeed. If husband or wife fail to do his or her part, adieu to the prospect of affinities. Neither husband or wife, single-handed and alone, can create affinities. If they are moral Samsons in outside effort, and can pull down solid temples of sin with single, unaided strength, in the hands of a treacherous Delilah, which notorious in-

dividual may prove to be a perverse disposition of
their own, they become as weak to create affinities
in their household as the Israelitish giant became
under the scissors of his wife.

Mrs. Squire Stebbins put on the handsomest bonnet, as directed, and revolved slowly in a circle, several times before the gaze of her admiring spouse,
so that she and her bonnet might be viewed from all
points.

" That 'll do, Ducky ; now take a look at yourself
in the glass."

She obeyed, and gave one searching look at the
model she displayed to herself by reflection.

" Is n't it superb, Hubby ? " she asked.

" I see two superbs, Mollie ! "

" Counting myself and the bonnet ?   The bonnet
first.   Does it suit you, Hubby ? " she replied.

" Does it suit you, Mollie ? "

" Yes, I think it is the sweetest thing I ever saw."

" That was n't human ? " asked the Squire.

" Yes, that was n't human ; I sha'n't be ashamed to
wear that bonnet anywhere."   Then she turned to
me.   " I am going to New York by and by.   My
husband is going, and he thinks he can't go anywhere without me, and I like to look well on his account.   I like to make him proud of me ; and I am
glad he thinks he can't go without me."

" Eh, Mollie ; or do you like to go with me and
show yourself off ? "

" If it pleases you to have me go, and to see me
show myself off, I do."

" How much is that gew-gaw ? " he asked me.

I told him. He took out his purse and handed me the money.

" I 'll make you a present of that bonnet, Mollie. I suppose that is what you brought me here for. I mistrusted, when you invited me to come with you, that your purse was getting light."

" No indeed ; I 've plenty ! " and she shook a well-filled purse before his eyes ; " but I accept the present with many thanks."

" No doubt ; you are very welcome," he said with a bow of mock politeness. Then turning to me he added, " I thought this a stratgeic manœuvre to let me know she was out of funds. Such hints are usually given, when the tide has nearly ebbed, and she is almost ashore."

" Is n't it a good fortune to be obliged to give nothing but hints in that quarter ? " she asked me.

May that couple never hide their conjugal candle under a bushel. May it be set up before the world and burn, and give light to all people that dwell in this great temple of married life.

The performance for this day is over.

XV.

I was obliged to descend from the mountain Ebenezer whereon I was perched yesterday, far above the storms and hurricanes of life. To-day I have had the common elements of humanity to deal with again. I bade adieu to the heights with regret: I held glorious revel there, too glorious to be of long continuance.

There is no position, unless it is when one is in love, where the female dual can so set forth the character to the observation of her fellows as in shopping. The performance of that necessary duty requires the quintessence of stratagem put forth in the most delicate manner to accomplish selfish ends successfully. Indeed, managing traders is very much like managing lovers, so far as obtaining the end sought is accomplished.

It can safely be averred of traders that, as a class, they are violently enamored of their profits.

A highway robber would be met more cordially, and esteemed more highly by those with whom he has to do, than a highway shopper, because the highwayman openly and avowedly violates the laws of decency and honesty in taking by force what belongs to another, and the highway shopper puts on airs of innocence and respectability while he docs the same thing.

No one would be willing to be classed among the ostracized gentry, richly as he might, in the esteem of the trader, deserve the distinction ; but many a tradesman or woman would be most happy to furnish the uniform, provided it could, like States-prison habiliments, indicate offenders to all observers.

If there were a ready-made clothing store established to accommodate customers of that description, what a scrambling there would be among neighbors to fit each other, suggests the inner.

I have had a great many examples of that kind presented to my observation, but it is not exactly of a highway shopper that I am going to tell you, my Journal ; the customer would figure to a little better advantage in the burglary troop. Her onslaught was more upon goods than profits.

My trial to-day came in the shape of a young lady from the country. She was in town to make a visit, and came in the store to buy mamma a cap. Every thing I had made up was too dear, and not of the right form. Mamma was an invalid, did n't go out at all; therefore it was unnecessary to have any thing dressy or expensive. She had lost her hair in one place, and required a particular form of cap to conceal the misfortune. She selected her materials, described the form of cap required, limited the price, and left.

In the afternoon she came back, examined the cap,

said it would do nicely for what mamma wanted ;
took it, and paid for it.   In about two hours she returned with a young lady friend, and the cap.

She showed it to me, and said it did n't exactly
suit.

" I will make any change you desire," I said " although it would have saved me trouble to have had
it done before it went out of the store."

" Oh no ! I could n 't think of putting you to that
trouble," she disclaimed earnestly.

" Then I don't know as any thing can be done
about it," I replied.

I saw that she wished me to take the cap, and return her the money ; but I did n't propose to do so,
for reasons which must be evident to any one of
common sense.

" Let us go up and see if mamma has n't something by which to alter it," proposed the accompany-
ing friend.

They left, and went up town, or professed to do
so. The longer I stay in business the more suspi-
cious I grow of professions. In a very short time
they returned. If they went up town, up-town
mamma had nothing as a pattern by which to alter it.

Both stood looking the poor offending cap over.
" It really did n't suit her ! "

I understood that she had found something somewhere else that suited her better. Perhaps up-town
mamma had an old-fashioned cap that she wished to

dispose of to a country relation. Whatever the other circumstance might be I was confident she wished me to take the cap, and give her the money; but I stood silent to let her propose it.

" I should n't think of asking you to take it back," she said, hesitatingly.

" Certainly not! " I replied. " It is one of my rules never to take a piece of cut goods back. If I were to do it, my ribbons and laces would be separated into inch bits, and left on my hands. Inexperienced as you are, you can see that that would n't do."

" But I really did n't see how it was going to look before it was made. How could I tell till I saw it ? "

" But it would n't do for us to cut up our goods in making experiments for you to see."

" But I am not suited in the cap."

" You selected your own materials, described the form, and limited the price. For so small a sum, out of so scanty materials, we could n't make a pretty cap; but we did the best we could. You had the thing in your own hands from the beginning; I don't see that we are in fault about it."

" I know you are not," she replied, and they went out again for a few moments, but returned shortly as dissatisfied as ever.

" It really don't suit me! would n't you be good enough to take it again ? "

I explained to her that the lace and ribbon, being cut, were spoiled to sell.

" But you are always selling caps," she urged.

" Certainly; but I should never make a cap in that form to sell; it is unfashionable. Nor should I think of making a cap of such ordinary materials to put in the store. I could n't sell it if I did. That cap was made to fit your mother's head, which is a peculiar head, and her taste, which is a peculiar taste. If I were to take it, and make it over for the store, there would be a waste of time and the material that would make it an utter loss. Indeed it is so cut up that I could n't make a cap at all, — it is too broad at the top, and too narrow at the bottom."

" You are always using pieces of lace," she persisted.

" Yes. and I make plenty without buying them. Are you not constantly requiring pieces of lace? most ladies are. It was cut up, and made unsalable through your mistake, not mine. If you make a mistake, it is for you to bear the consequence of it. Don't you see what you are doing when you wish to make me bear the expense of your mistakes?" I asked this in sham surprise that she should desire so unheard-of a thing. I was not surprised; nor should I be at any thing that might be asked of me, if it were to give away a bill of sale of my goods with myself included.

She could see nothing but that she wished me to take the cap, and return her the money. The enormous amount of one dollar seventy-five cents was the sum in contention. She acknowledged the fault

to be hers, but, woman-like, she could n't carry out
the reasoning that followed practically, that it was her
place to bear the loss.

She had made up her mind to sponge, — yes, hard
as the word is, there is such a word in unadulterated
Anglo-Saxon, and if there is such a word it was
made to be used, and if it was made to be used it
never was more applicable than in this connection,—
she intended to sponge that dollar seventy-five cents
out of me. I had arrived at an equally decided conclusion that I would n't stand sponging. Not that I
cared for the trifling sum of money, I had far sooner
given it her than suffer the annoyance she had made
me; but I intended to exercise my free moral
agency in bestowing my charity, not upon her, but
where I chose. The fact is, I had got my back up
by her behavior, and would neither be driven or
coaxed. I was in no mood to give my cloak when
my coat was taken. In fact, I was in no mood to
give up my coat peaceably.

I was thoroughly indignant! How that dollar
seventy-five cents must have grown and enlarged in
her view as she dwelt upon its departure. " How
blessings brighten as they take their flight." How
it diminished, growing smaller and smaller, and beautifully less in my esteem as I regarded it to be her
loss.

" Still, I would rather make a sacrifice on the cap
than keep it," she urged.

She probably saw my emotions as through a glass

darkly. I had become exasperated, lost my temper;
or become nervous, as delicate individuals report
themselves when they get out of humor; I would n't
take the ill-favored thing at any rate. I can't de-
scribe to you, dear Journal, how ugly that cap had
come to look in my eyes. I would n't have continued it in my sight a moment, only that I was
obliged to endure it. If she had left it, as her
threatening looks portended, I should have taken
the poker to the odious thing, and hustled it uncere-
moniously into the obscure quarters which we denominate the rag bag.

"Then, my dear child," I said, oiling the outside of
the tart rejoinder with gentleness, "you had better
make the sacrifice by taking the cap, and saying no
more about it."

I really pitied the ignorance in which she had
been educated, and I thought I would make one
more effort to explain the state of the case by illustration.

"You would n't think of buying a dress, having
it made up, then returning to the store where you
bought it, and ask them to take it again because
you had changed your mind?" I said.

"That would be a different thing," she replied.

"A difference without distinction. One garment
would be a cap, the other a dress. If your money
is of value to you, this will be a good lesson to teach
you how to spend it. You will hereafter look around,
see what there is in the market, and determine what

you want, without asking milliners to cut up their goods in experimenting for your benefit. Instead of trying to make other people make up for your losses, and suffer for your ignorance, you will bear them silently at the time, and learn wisdom from them for the future."

Perhaps she will be profited by my advice, and the occasion of it.

When the young lady found it impossible to induce me to pay for her mistake, she took up the offending bone of contention, and left without even inclining her head in valedictory of departure. But the young lady who was with her did n't deign to let me off so politely. She turned round, and with a significant nod fretted out, —

" You can do as you please ; but you will be sorry for being so disobliging. It does n't do for shopkeepers to be too independent."

Her remark signified to me that she would take her revenge by injuring my reputation as a shop-keeper. The poor little simpleton really thought that she was impressing me with the necessity of being more amiable to my customers. Instead, she was actually stamping her inner character upon her outside manners. I set her down as possessing a disposition to make arbitrary exactions of black mail wherever she could succeed. The petty tyranny being successfully resisted, she would revenge the abortion of her attempt by injuring me all in her power.

If the young lady castigate my back, in my

absence, I refuse to smart under the rod. I have so long belonged to the suffering class of humanity that suffering has become my normal condition.

If she flourish in the vocation of reporter, those who hear to understand and remember her "jottings," will be of her own kind. "Birds of a feather flock together." In that case an overruling Hand may bring good out of evil. To save one dollar seventy-five cents, in an ordinary numerical calculation upon such customers, might in the course of time, a century or two, become quite a stock in trade, and give my great-great-grand-children the eclat of belonging to one of the first families.

If the wrath of that young woman can't be made to praise me in any way, I count myself competent to praise myself in her behalf. Which benevolent undertaking I accomplish by saying, that I am possessed of that desirable equanimity of temper that refuses to allow itself to be disturbed in consequence of becoming the subject of any such sensational items as she may see fit to put in circulation.

In the conscious rectitude of my side of the story I tranquilly repose. If a lie will go around the world while the truth is pulling his boots on, deliberate as his action may be, the truth is sure to follow.

In view of the following statement, a few remarks may be profitable, by way of inference and improvement.

When the young lady wished me to take back the cap, she was spending my money: when she was obliged to keep it, she was spending her own.

I have observed that one of the easiest things in the world to accomplish is the spending of other people's money. I have seen a man sit down, take his pencil and paper, and spend his neighbor's whole fortune with one or two dashes of black lead. I have seen him buy his neighbor an estate, furnish his house, supply his larder, fill his stable, regulate his charities, coolly distribute a million or so, without causing a single pang to rend his own heart at the parting. Generous man! But when it comes to spending one's own, — aye, there is the hitch!

In the same spirit, I have seen one brother bear another brother's reverses and bereavements.

I have seen a whole circle of friends bear up under the afflictions of one friend's family with a fortitude and resignation worthy to be held up as an example for the imitation of all observers.

It is truly astonishing how much human nature will endure without murmuring, when it is afflicted in behalf of others!

XVI.

JUDGE MAY came in this morning, and paid Rose's bill. I ventured to ask, I was so anxious to know, —

" Did the bonnet suit ? "

" Perfectly, I think ; I heard no fault expressed," he answered.

I asked again, " All round ? "

" All round," he replied, " I liked it. It looked like Rosie. Mrs. May is not quite well to-day, or she would have been down herself, and as several days may elapse before she gets round she asked me to step in and pay you. She dislikes very much to have a little bill standing."

" Tell her, if you please, that I am obliged to her for feeling so; not that I need the money," I added quickly, fearing he might think I did from my eagerness in speaking.

" I understand ; you like the principle of promptness. We know that you may have the opportunity to use the money two or three times in as many days, and get your interest every time you use it, if we pay you when your bill is due. If it lies idle in our purse " —

" Our purse ! " I echoed, I could n't help it. I was startled out of all propriety by the expression, and my voice rang through the room in a scream of surprise.

The Judge took, entered into the spirit of my idea, and laughed heartily. I was ashamed of myself. I could only blush and simper like a little girl.

" Yes, it is *our* purse at *our* house. We know so long as we neglect to pay you, we are keeping you out of the use of your money."

Your money! Human nature, your redemption draweth nigh! it is at hand; it is here! We are affinities, — Judge May whom I have seen, and Mrs. Judge May whom I have not seen! Our spirits assimilate if we never meet in the flesh. Whoever before thought of calling a milliner's money hers till she got it, even if that desirable event delay transpiring on this side the River.

A word to the wise is sufficient, and Judge May has said that word in favor of prompt payments.

Judge May had scarcely passed out of the door when two shadows darkened it. No, those two ladies did not darken the door, they only turned down the light that came in through it.

Human transparencies! no oils of gladness could have painted the lights and shadows which made your images stand out on the canvas of life! Lean, lank, cadaverous, hungry-looking mortals! are you human? or are you galvanized skeletons dressed up to personify Want? You must be human women, or you would never be around looking after such gear as I keep for the adornment of flesh and blood. If

10

you are from the nether regions, the ruling passion
had strength enough in you—poor woman's foible!—
to form a line of communication between this world
and the other to bring you back shopping.

Here, on the surface, appears — to look deeper into it it might be doubtful about the fact holding together — a remedy for the necessary idleness of a
large class of women in the Beyond. There being
no millinery or dry-goods stores on the other side,
to afford them occupation and entertainment, idleness, the prolific source of evil, must ensue, and unlimited mischief, as a legitimate result, be concocted
there.

I establish the proposition that many a woman
must be idle in the future life, by an allowable process of reasoning. In this life her whole education
and occupation has been dress. Spiritual employments have been unlearned, unpracticed; therefore,
she must, per force, be idle unless she find some
means to follow her old occupation. The force of
habit is allowed, by all observers, to be the greatest
mental assistance which advanced age employs in
performing the occupations of life; therefore it is
no fair inference to suppose a woman will form new
tastes, and enter new occupations after she has spent
a lifetime in forming the habit of following one particular one.

Now if her inexhaustible, imperishable love of dress
can be taken with her, — love is an element of the
soul in its vitality, — who knows, since the wonderful
success of telegraphic inventions, what human skill

may be able to accomplish! Who knows but some ingenious human being may be able to form a line of communication between woman's love of dress on the other side, and milliners' stores, whose eternal doom is to revel on this! Should that be so, I shall set no magnets to attract my old customers. I see a possible difficulty in the way of trading with them. I am not acquainted with the currency of spiritual green-backs, and I am at a little loss to know how my profits would be dispensed.

In looking over the walking phenomena supposed to be human duals, I discovered them to be made up on very good frames. The coverings, if they had been brushed up with a little paint, would have been presentable. They really proved to be genuine frames and coverings, in despite of my forebodings. The greatest deficiency which presented itself to my examination was a lack of stuffing, which might be denominated plumpness, that part of the female corporate which flatterers denominate its "rounded, beautiful outline." Cotton, in very minute quantities, supplied, or attempted to supply, the deficiency. But cotton is too expensive an article to be consumed for the purely artistic purpose of embellishment in creating symmetric proportions; therefore it had been used sparingly.

Hunger, or gentility, I could hardly decide which, was written all over them. To my reading it was hunger. How I longed to take them home, and give them six months' board, or what would be an improvement on my good intentions, get them a seat at Squire Stebbins' table, with a dessert of his little chuckle turned into rounds of hearty laughter. It may be vulgar to eat heartily, and it may be vulgar to laugh heartily; but both exercises, properly regulated, are conducive to good health, and consequently good looks. What more powerful motive could be placed before a woman to induce her to commit both vulgarities?

Those anatomies came to get a piece of green ribbon, in the enormous quantity of one yard, to make a bow. The cost was one shilling a yard.

They seated themselves before the counter with the due solemnity required by the occasion, uncased their hands, and laid their gloves carefully down. Then they deliberately examined the ribbon which I put before them, comparing the different pieces, and descanting on the quality of each. When they had decided which to take they began to cheapen it. I made that a rapid proceeding. I would have given all the green ribbon I had to see them vanish, like Macbeth's ghost, into thin air. I had no fault to find with their thinness, they were successful competitors for ghostly honors in that respect.

I was chilled through! My teeth chattered! In another moment I should have been frozen into an icicle, or a statue, or an ice-cream, lacking the condiments.

When they took their departure I never exactly knew, but my ears were subjected to a visitation of creaking which I supposed came from their joints as they moved over the floor. When I ventured to look they were gone.

A year has been added to my age in a day, which elongation was produced by the awful solemnities of that green ribbon occasion.

When I revived, I took the whole matter under consideration, and pity supplanted horror in my emotions. That shows to a demonstration the expulsive power of a new emotion. A parallel may very properly be applied to the affections, and thus save pages of theological discussion, if theologians would avail themselves of my discovery.

My pity was not of that character which is nearly allied to love, it was nearer akin to fear. In my girlhood I suffered shockingly through the instrumentality of two respectable unmarried ladies of unmentionable age, who looked and acted precisely like the two who came in to-day.

O memory! thy capacity is powerful for good or evil! Is it possible thou wilt condescend to lend thyself to the naughty purpose of keeping that old spite alive in my heart! Shocking perversion of a noble faculty!

XVII.

THAT precious, invaluable little dual, that pearl of womanity, Mrs. Quickly, came in this afternoon to leave her orders. I had been fretted to death, and was at cross purposes with all womankind, but she set me right in a moment. Her bright, cheerful face is a beam of sunshine wherever it shows itself. Her salutation was a cheery, musical, —

" Good afternoon! and a right good afternoon it is! I wish you were at liberty to go out, and drink in the fresh air as I have done. It is more invigorating than wine!"

In my heart I echoed the wish. I did n't like to express it, but as the novelty of my new employment wears off I begin to feel the confinement of it. I am afraid my adventure in trade will prove more irksome than amusing to me. I begin to see how constant delving wears into the muscles and the spirit. The kind of necessity that controls one is of little consequence. It is the relentless *must be* that binds him down to his especial care, which proves the galling, cankering fetter. The invisible band is always pressing upon the muscles of the poor; it presses upon the muscles of the rich. Who-

ever lives is, in some way, the bond-slave of necessity, — a master that forever points the thong and
drives the lash.

"How tiresome it must be standing here, talking
bonnets, all day; I will be as expeditious as possible,
but I must tire you a little more. I have three jobs
on my hands, and I must shift them on yours," she
said briskly.

"I am here on purpose to be tired that way," I
replied.

"I know, but that does n't make it any more
pleasant to be tied in-doors this fine weather. It
is very agreeable to work when one likes, and play
when one likes, but it is the lot of few."

"Household duties tie you to the same care, only
it allows of a little different arrangement when one
wishes for recreation or rest," I replied philosophi-
cally. I was intent upon mastering my discontent,
or at least concealing it.

"Yes, the cares of a family are just as unflinching,
and peremptory in their calls as yours; but, as you
say, some things can be put by so that I can get
rest if I need, or recreation if I please. They are
not burdensome cares to me, because they are to my
taste. I like housekeeping. There is an exhilera-
tion in the exercise of sweeping, dusting, and cook-
ing that is very agreeable. Then, it is so pleasant to
see things nicely done. And it creates a proud, satisfied feeling to see something accomplished."

"I think that most women like housekeeping, un-

less their tastes have been perverted by false sentiments.   And it is one of the Father's wise provisions that it is so.   Still, there are exceptions.   There
are those with whom housekeeping is not a born
vocation, and cannot be acquired.   Individual capacity ought to be consulted as much in a woman's
choice of occupation as in a man's."

"Certainly; and I was about to say, no woman
ought to marry unless her vocation is for housekeeping; but it would have been a very thoughtless remark, there is so much involved in marriage beside
that."

"But when a woman marries she ought to cultivate a taste for housekeeping above all other employments.   I am not a born housekeeper.   It requires
double the study and care for me to manage a house
well that it does to do many other things which
might be considered quite out of a woman's sphere.
But I had the ambition to do well what I undertook;
so by giving it a great deal of attention I became a
tolerable housekeeper.   It was far more fatiguing
and perplexing than my present business, take as
much pains as I would to learn the best ways of doing it."

"Now, for the bonnets;" said Mrs. Quickly.
"First comes my important self.   Because I take
precedence of the rest of the family in rank, I must
be attended to first to maintain my dignity."

That was an old-fashioned sentiment; but the
lady who adopted it understood its value, and

cherished it for its own sake. She was no echo of fashionable sentiments. Good, sound common sense was the basis of her character, and good principles governed her actions.

Mrs. Lacker came up to the counter just then, and overhearing the last part of Mrs. Quickly's remark, asked, —

"What were you saying, — that you get your own things done first?"

"Yes, that is my way," answered Mrs. Quickly.

"It is n't mine. I look out for all the rest first, and leave myself till the last."

Mrs. Lacker said this with an air of profound self-satisfaction, — with the pride of humility that finds exaltation in self-abasement; or in what it persuades itself is self-abasement. The human heart is so deceitful above all things, and so desperately wicked, that its motives need carefully looking into before any course of action is adopted.

"It is proper that you should look out for your equals first; that is the place of your husband in the family; I think he should always be considered first; put do you put your children before yourself?"

"Yes, I am obliged to attend to them first, or I should have no peace to do my own things."

"Is n't it your place to regulate your children in such a way as always to have peace to do what is needful? Are you not afraid, by putting yourself below your children in those respects which stand out so prominent in a family, that you will give them an advantage over you, and such a low estimate of you, that they will fail to pay you the respect and deference which is due a parent from a child? It is necessary to count in all these little things to make the sum come right when it is added up."

May your lesson be blessed, was the echo of the inner. It is the right principle to advocate and practice in rearing children. I have seen it turned topsy-turvy so many years, mixed up and confused with ideas of the excellence and superiority of children, that I was delighted to see one mother travelling in the good old track of common sense, and divine command. A few such would be the salvation of the rising generation. Let us entreat that the number be multiplied, lest when inquisition be made among its mothers, like righteous Abraham's prayers to lessen the number requisite to save the whole from destruction, ours be unavailing to save our children from the consequences of our bad management.

"No!" said Mrs. Lacker emphatically: "I have no such fear. When I was young I could n't have any thing decent. Mother must have this and that, — she could n't afford me any thing; and I don't intend my children shall be mortified in that way. I always had to sit with my feet drawn up under my frock to hide my shabby boots. If I happened, by some inexplicable accident, to get a pretty frock, it must be set off with some faded or dyed-over ribbon to spoil my comfort in it, and make me miserable.

No, my children shall never go through such tortures to lay up against me when they grow up."

The lady had freed her mind undoubtedly; she had
also aired a pretty piece of family history that ac-
counted to her hearers for her one-sided views of
rearing children; but she did n't consider that.

"I hope if your mother did err, as perhaps she
might, on the side of strictness in dressing you in
your childhood, you have n't laid it up against her.
That would be in bad taste as well as bad temper.
To retaliate the wrong upon your children by going
to the other extreme would be still worse. I did n't
have all I wanted when I was a child; but I had
faith enough in my parents, and still have, to think
they got me all they could, or thought best for me to
have. If they erred toward me it was an error of
judgment, not of love. I could easily overlook it. If
I did n't I should expect my children to return me
the same measure. And nothing in life could pain
me so sorely as to have an unloving, thankless child.
Indeed I could n't allow it in my heart to blame my
parents, do as they might, much more take it upon
my lips," said Mrs. Quickly seriously.

"I can see that my mother was to blame, and I
don't see any harm in speaking of it." Mrs. Lacker
clung to her own ideas tenaciously, and saw fit to
express them, independently if not discreetly. But
it seemed strange to me that she did n't see and feel
the force of Mrs. Quickly's remarks. She was a
mother, where was her tenderness? how could she

bear to have a child speak of her as she had spoken of her mother before strangers ?

"The harm in speaking so," said Mrs. Quickly, " is that you dishonor your parent and disgrace yourself. And it seems to me that good taste. if not good principle, should lead one to pass by a parent's faults in silence." Mrs. Quickly knew she was speaking to one who had set God's commands at naught to follow modern revelations ; so she based her reply upon reasons that she thought might be appreciated.

" It is better to avoid extremes in all things," she went on; "but if either should be more carefully avoided in the case of children than the other, it should be the extreme of indulgence that is practiced nowadays. Without knowledge, without experience, without judgment, how can they be fit to rule and direct themselves or others. Who ever saw them become any thing but exacting, arbitrary, unreasonable masters. In the parents' old age, when they had been allowed the mastery in youth, I have seen their rule become intolerable. Not only indifference and neglect, but absolute cruelty practiced."

" That has happened where children are strictly brought up."

" Yes, on the other extreme. If children acquire a disrespect for parents, it is usually through some fault of the parents, I allow ; but how children can retain the feeling of resentment after they become parents is a mystery to me."

" All have more or less human nature in them," said Mrs. Lacker lightly; " children bring it into the world with them. I have no belief in whipping and scolding it out of them. Coaxing answers a better purpose."

" I know those are very common ideas; but for all that, I must cling to the precepts of my Bible, rather than be governed by precepts of man's wisdom. I think wholesome restraint is always necessary, and wholesome castigation well adapted to some circumstances. A wholesome authority should always be maintained by parents, tenderly but firmly, in order to command the respect of children."

" I hope you don't believe all the nonsense in that book you mentioned?" said Mrs. Lacker with a sneer.

" If you refer to the Bible, I do. Every word within its lids. There is much of it that I don't understand. I must accept the whole Bible, or reject the whole of it. I shouldn't know which part was truth, and which was falsehood. Indeed, I wouldn't be willing to take any book of precepts which was part a lie and part the truth to be my rule of life, and guide into eternity."

" And you believe blindly what you don't understand; that is truly sensible!"

" If I don't understand, it is owing to my lack of apprehension, no fault in the Book."

" Do you believe that silly story about Jonah's going into the belly of a whale, and staying three days and three nights?"

" It is n't silly to me. God says He uses simple
means to confound the wise ones of this world.
What would appear very trivial to one might prove
of great consequence to another. A profound thinker
discovered the law of gravitation by noticing so simple an incident as the falling of an apple. Many
very talented people would have failed to notice so
small a thing. Perhaps if we were to give as careful
study to God's laws, as we do to investigations of science, we might discern as wonderful things in them
as are continually unfolding themselves in science."

" How could Jonah breathe in the belly of a
whale ? "

" By the same miraculous power that made his
lungs and adapted them when he was not in the
whale to the use of the air and the air to their use,
could the Maker adapt Jonah to the condition he
was in, in the whale's belly. If I only believe what
I understand, I should n't believe my own existence.
I don't understand it."

During this conversation, a little woman in short
skirts and trousers, with her hair stringing in ropelets about her face, had stood behind Mrs. Lacker
listening. She now stepped up, and laid her hand
on that lady's shoulder. A few contortions con-
vulsed the muscles of her face, like the twitches oc-
casioned by the application of the electricity of the
galvanic battery, her eyes closed, and raising her
hand in oratoric flourish she exclaimed, —

" Deny not your faith, though temptation beset

you! Dare to be a woman! Fight for the right!
Be a woman in the strife! Be a hero in the strife,
and earn the reward promised to the faithful! Be
not an idler! be up and doing while the day lasts,
for the night cometh — the long dark night!"

Spirits it seemed were rampant in the midst, but
as I like to go to the bottom of things instead of
gliding smoothly on the current of unknown mean-
ings, I stopped her by telling her she had got beyond my depth. At first she took no notice of my
interruption, but I took up the yard-stick and touched
her elbow, just to command attention and enforce
my right to the floor. I told her I would like to
have her explain what she had already offered before
she went further. I wished to understand, like Mrs.
Lacker, before I believed.

" In the first place, what do you mean by 'daring
to be a woman?' Do you mean mentally, morally,
or physically? If physically, I don't see as the
power of choice is left her, she being a physiological
fact when she makes her *debut* on this mundane
sphere.

" What is it to be a woman morally? If you mean
to possess courage, and to exercise it in doing what
she considers right, various questions might arise
out of that position, such as, What would be right
under all circumstances? Would what would be
right at one time be right at all times? and so on.

" If you mean 'dare to be a woman' mentally, the
accomplishing of that aim depends upon whether

you can or not, from the provisions Nature has made, and art afforded. If Nature has endowed you with ordinary capacity, combined with a taste for intellectual employments, and industry to study, you may make quite an intellectual woman of yourself provided you have the facilities.

" What is it to 'be a hero in the strife'?   Do you mean to stir up strife? or to make confusion worse where it is stirred up?   There are already too many too well endowed with that capacity, without being invited to cultivate it.   It would be far more in accordance with the proper ideal of woman to incite peace-making propensities.

"'Fight' what, or for what? If you mean fight with her fists, or with her tongue, the ability to do either is a very undesirable accomplishment for a woman. If you mean that she should fight her own evil disposition till she brings it under subjection, so as to set good examples in an upright life and well-ordered conversation, I would say, may your teaching be sped for good.

"'Be up and doing!' up where? doing what? If you mean up in the morning doing with the might what the hands find to do, I agree with you. If you mean, up in the pulpit holding forth precepts for others to practice, that is another thing. If you mean up, setting up impious doctrines against the Maker of all men, stirring up doubts in the minds of the ignorant, or ambitions in the minds of those who will subvert good principles for the honors of leadership, I demur. Now before you proceed in your exhortation, please make what you have said plain to the discernment of wayfaring people."

" There are adverse, trifling spirits here," she said, " I can do nothing." A few little shivers disturbed her muscles, and the "influence" took summary leave of us. Whence it came or whither it went I know not.

" Grieve not the spirits," was the solemn admonition that issued in deep, sepulchral tones from the depths of the departing ropelets.

" How very easy it is for superstitious minds to be overcome by that remarkable phenomenon called Mesmerism," said Mrs. Quickly.

" Some people get hold of one idea that has truth for its foundation, the spiritual nature of man partaking of God's nature as a spiritual existence, and then, unwilling to wait and study into the mysteries of the spiritual element of creation, they try, through the phenomenon we have just witnessed, to leap into the heart of eternity, and fathom its mysteries."

" There is something strange and mysterious in it."

" Yes, and so there is in the phenomenon of sleep. Who can understand the state of the mind, or the body either, when in that unconscious condition. It is ignorance, self-conceit, and vaunting ambition that makes so much mischief out of that peculiar phenomenon which we just witnessed. Now let us go back to bonnets, if this episode is finished."

11

" Show me a shade of golden brown silk. I have made up my mind to have a silk one, and I must make it answer all purposes."

I placed several shades of brown silk before her. and named their prices.

" I like that shade," she said, pointing to a rich lustrous silk ; " but it will make my bonnet come a little higher than I intended ; so I will have it made of that ; " and she laid out a piece of inferior quality. "I will have buff trimmings to go with it, only a facing of blue. I must always have a tinge of blue to clear my complexion ; but keep it out of sight as much as possible. Now show me flowers and ties to compare with the silk. I have some lace that I will send in. Make me as pretty a bonnet as you can out of these materials. Put the bows as low on the top as possible, because I am tall, and I don't wish to add to my height, — a little on one side, to make them look easy."

" You shall have just as pretty a bonnet as I can make," I said ; and I mentally added, the time you have saved in giving your order shall be bestowed upon your bonnet.

" Now comes Jennie next in order, as she is the eldest daughter. She has decided to have a little jaunty hat, and wear it everywhere for the present. The one she tried yesterday ; you laid it aside for her, she said. Trim it up with the ribbon and grass she looked at. If you don't remember I'll tell you her description."

" I remember ; " little should I forget the orders of such customers.

" No doubt you will suit her ; she described what she wanted."

" If it don't exactly suit when it is finished, she can step in, and we will alter it."

" Now comes Baby Nell, and her order is the prettiest hat in town. Her father says, the very prettiest."

What a volume that one sentence, " her father says," unfolded. I saw the proud, protective love that swelled his heart toward that baby girl. The little image hovering around his day's work, to make toil lighter ; meeting his homeward steps to rob them of fatigue ; hovering around his pillow, to make sleep sweet. Mysterious tie of blessed paternal love !

" Fit up the little jockey I looked at yesterday in just the cunningest manner in the world, — with puffs of illusion filled with those dainty moss-rose buds. Make it look like a fairy's crown. Use every thing you need, whether I have selected it or not. Her father will allow no stint on Pet's hat, if he works night and day to get the money to pay for it."

" What a blessed customer ! " said I to Gracie.

" Yes, and many would make a good thing out of such loose orders."

I took, but the insinuation angered me.

" Whoever would take advantage of such a customer is a disgrace to the calling ! " I said · indignantly.

"No doubt the calling is often so disgraced," replied Grace coolly. "Those that do it would say she has plenty."

"If she has plenty it is n't mine but hers to do with as she pleases. And that some do take advantage, whenever they can, is one reason that customers haggle and banter as they do, and mistrust us all. I wish all who trade in that way had to take the trouble they make the rest of us."

I strongly suspect there is blame on both sides for the haggling and bantering of customers, — for the present status of trade. The fault is not all on one side, nor all from one motive. Avarice sometimes rules; but usually selfishness is figuring to secure as much as possible for as small an amount of money as can be laid out. The multitude are struggling from necessity, to get a living, and the motive that prompts the management to get a good trade is the desire to obtain a decent, respectable living among one's fellows.

Pride aggravates the trouble between buyers and sellers by prompting some to adopt comforts and luxuries superior to their neighbors.

Pride is the occasion of more dishonesty than avarice, and necessity is the prolific parent of meanness.

XVIII.

June 8, 18—.

I suppose I have lost a customer; but in view of that shocking result of my conduct, I remain in a state of hardened indifference as to the consequences.

I promised Mrs. Mann her bonnet at eight o'clock this evening. She came in at five, and said she was going to ride. She would n't be home until ten, — her house would be locked up while she was gone, — she would call on her return, and take it.

I replied, "The store will be locked up before ten."

"What! locked up before ten o'clock! I thought all milliners worked till twelve Saturday night."

"I am an exception to that rule. I shut up at the usual hour Saturday night."

She looked at me with as much astonishment as one would look upon a menagerie of imported animals, and then said, —

"If you must go home, one of the girls can wait till I come back."

"No, ma'am; I send my contrabands home to get the same rest that I need myself. None of them can stay here two or three hours after their time, to deliver your bonnet."

" Leave it here, and I 'll send down in the morning, and get it."

" No, ma'am; I don't work seven days in the week. If God's laws did not forbid it, the laws for preserving health do. Six days out of seven are enough for any one to work."

" I don't think it would be much just to run down here in the morning, and hand out a bonnet."

" But it would be just enough to break up my morning, and bring week-day employments before my mind. I wish to dismiss them entirely from my thoughts on Sunday."

I might have told her that I occupied them with other things, so as to get as perfect a rest from business vexations as possible, but there is another motive of more consequence still. To have mentioned it to her would have been unnecessary. Those who love to think of the wonderful things of creation, and of the soul, and learn about them, can understand it. One day out of seven is little time enough for such comfort.

" Other milliners work Saturday night, and send bonnets Sunday morning. I can't go to meeting unless I have it."

That continual quoting of other milliners to me! I am tired to death of hearing it. I cannot regulate myself by other people's consciences. But that is the rule of the multitude. " Measuring themselves by themselves " throngs pass on through life to Life; and The Standard for moral action remains unstudicd, unpracticed. Why is it? Introduced into life, it is, and must be evermore around them. After this the inevitable, endless future! Still they go on through this to that, huddled together, doing one as the other, an unthinking mass, till they arrive at the dark valley! Then they go on alone in their glory or their folly, — to what? God knows. Would that the startling picture faced them, haunted them in the press and rush of present travel, so that they could not avoid thinking of it. In the valley there is no retreat to make a change. The sum of life is made up, and it is made up of such little items as buying, making, selling, and wearing a bonnet.

The last argument, no doubt, Mrs. Mann thought was irresistible. She could n't present herself in God's house to perform His worship unless she and I both violated His laws. The mockery, the sham of worship could not be performed before the All-seeing Eye without the aid of a new bonnet! His attention and admiration included were to be propitiated by a new fashion in dress! Poor, short-sighted Deity! — Deity unable to penetrate farther than the outside covering of the head! — a God truly worthy of a fashionable woman's worship!

If she wanted the bonnet for a covert from justly aroused wrath, it were becoming to have her head covered. With flowers and ribbons? It would n't matter. The gay garment may become sackcloth in His sight if the heart is humble. But, alas, is it not one part of the pantomime of sham worship to frizzle and bedeck and put on airs, — for whose eye? that of one's fellows. For whose worship? that of the unique individual called I. What is it named? God's service. That the Father's heart is strong with love and pity for the children worshipers that fall down before him in their shamming, and pride, and ambition, and worldly folly, God be praised.

The eye of the inner dual went out, and looked over the great congregation where that woman worships, — the largest, richest, and most fashionable one in town, — so she boasts.

Alas for God's worship! Every god, of every shape except the Unknown God, was set up in every separate heart. The idol self sat enthroned the god of gods, bedecked in the frivolity of costly apparel. Individual pride for individual self, and banded pride for the fashionable church; and God the Father had withered to a pulpless husk, a wind-inflated effigy of a human imagination of greatness.

Sadly I felt, severely I 've no doubt I spoke, low it must have been, my throat was swollen and full. I grew so hoarse I could hardly utter, but I said it: —

" Other milliners cannot become my standard. I can pin my faith to no such sleeve. If other milliers can go to judgment for me, and render my account for obedience or disobedience to my Maker's law, — if they can do that I will allow them to regulate my actions. When other milliners will take the responsibility of securing to myself, and those I have charge of, an unbroken constitution, and a conscience void of offense, they may regulate my habits of labor. If you will tell me where I can send your bonnet at eight to-night, I will send it, and you can get it when you please."

"You are very precise! I don't think you will increase your trade much by being so very strict! You can send my bonnet to the store, No. 8 Exchange Street, with the bill!" and with a fiery red face she tore herself away.

Gracie came round to me and whispered : —

"She made all that flourish to get rid of the bill; but she thought you understood her, so she did n't carry it out." Naughty Gracie! "Of course you could n't be so wicked as to take pay for a bonnet Sunday morning if you delivered it. If she had come in at ten to-night she would have been in such a hurry she would have forgotten it, or forgotten her purse, or had some accident ready for the occasion. I'll take the bonnet round when I go to tea; but I sha'n't leave it unless I get the pay."

"You should never give one such a name unless you know it to be true, Gracie."

"I do know it to be true! I have collected bills there before. I had a deal of trouble one time, in getting a bill I carried there to collect. The clerk refused to pay it. I told him it was Mrs. Mann's orders to have it sent there. He said he was n't employed by Mrs. Mann, and he had orders to pay no bill till Mr. Mann saw it. If he had told me he had orders to pay no bill that could possibly be got rid of, he would have told the truth. That is the name they have all over town."

" Well, how did you come out?" I asked.

" I waited till Mr. Mann came in, just as I was directed to. He swore at first he would n't pay it; but I told him it would be collected some other way if he did n't, — his wife had the goods. It would have made your ears tingle the way he swore about her. If you get rid of her by the way you talked to her, you will be fortunate. She has just about as much sense of shame as he."

JUNE 10, 18—.

The store has been full of lookers since we got in our new stock of goods. " We did n't come to buy, we only came to look; we want to see what you have," is the general remark. It is shockingly tiresome, this showing goods; but one of the necessary evils of trade. If some make it an opportunity to gossip, it can't very well be helped. The more people that are drawn to the store the more prospect of custom. The habit of coming is the first step to trading.

" Such an one has so-and-so, at such a price," said one lady to another to-day: " I think you had better go there and see their goods before you buy." I thought, if you were in my place how would you like to have me sit in your store, and advise your customers to go somewhere else and buy. She did n't think. Such thoughtlessness was unpardonable.

The lady advised saw the color come and go in my face, as I strove to control myself, and she said, — " No matter now. I 'm not going to buy for a few days."

The adviser had no such aptitude to understand another's feelings, and she went on, " Go there by all means before you buy."

The advised was fretted by her want of tact, or rather good manners, and she said pointedly, —

" You don't intend to disparage the goods here by recommending them elsewhere ; but it might be so taken by this lady, and she will consider it hardly fair for you to sit in her store and advertise for another at her expense."

" I was only looking out for you," the other replied.

A look was the answer. It was a look which said, If you please, exercise a little more good taste as well as good sense about it.

The lady who sat in my store, to advise people to go to other places to buy, was a compound of effrontery and ignorance, said Resentment. Wink ! said Charity.

XIX.

POOR little Annie Drew came in this morning. She is very pale, and thin, and worn out looking. We were school-girls together. Then, she was plump, rosy, beautiful with health and happiness.

What ails you, Annie? was the question of the inner as I looked at her. I must know. Her husband lifted her from the carriage as tenderly as he would an infant, and set her inside the door. There can be no trouble in that quarter.

The more I looked at her the more I wondered. Her muscles were consumed. Her skin dry, lifeless, withered. Her blood was colorless, exhausted. Her limbs were limp and without vigor.

The outer store was no place in which to talk with her, and I took her into my own room.

Before her husband left he came up to her and said, "Now, Annie, make yourself look as well as you can. If you only looked as nice, and plump, and fair, as your friend here, I'd give half I'm worth. Get a bonnet that will make you look as young and fresh as you can."

I saw a mist gather over Annie's eyes, and a teardrop form, but she smiled as she answered, —

"Yes, George; I'll do my best."

I was repelled; more, I was angered. His compliment at his wife's expense was disgusting. I was angry that he could suppose me capable of enjoying or even tolerating it. I forgot that as he is in his heart he judges me to be, and addresses me accordingly. Tenderly as he had taken care of Annie, he had given her a thrust that had cut her to the heart. I could n't help thinking, — How could she fancy him ?

We went into my room together, and sat down side by side, and put our arms about each other in silence for a few moments. Then we talked of old times, as old school-mates will talk, till an hour had passed away. Then, Annie said, —

"I must be looking for a bonnet. George will be back soon, and I must be ready for him. Make me look just as well as possible, dear; I know I am all faded out, — it is sickness, and the care of children. I would be glad to look young and fair as I used, but I can't. The care of the children wears me out, and I must take care of them, and it spoils my good looks."

"George looks as though he might bear some of the burden, and lighten your cares."

"He does, — he pities me."

On the impulse, I put my arms around her as we stood, and drew her head to my shoulder, and whispered, — "He loves you?"

"He pities me," she repeated in a weary tone,

and the hot tears rolled over her cheeks. "How can he love me when I have grown so plain and helpless?"

"It is his duty; you have worn yourself out for him and his," I exclaimed passionately.

"So far he does. Duty may point the way; but love refuse to follow his bidding. We love what is desirable in our sight, — what excites love. I can't be to George what I used, and I can't expect him to feel toward me as he used. He gives me all I can command. He don't know how it hurts my feelings when he compares me with finer-looking women to my disadvantage."

I was in possession of the whole story. At a glance I saw to the bottom of her unhappiness. Her beauty had been consumed with passion, and the man's eyes were unsatisfied, and had wandered off in the love of change. Annie, in the consciousness of her waning beauty, had meekly borne it, and pined.

I thought I saw a remedy for a part of the trouble, at least. He might be broken of putting the change in her looks so constantly before her, and in consequence making her so unhappy. All the time she was selecting her bonnet the inner was at work upon the idea.

When she left I said, —

"I am going up to spend a Sabbath with you in a week or two."

"George will come down for you Saturday night."

"Yes, that I will, Annie. Her cheerful face in the house will well repay the trouble. Let it be next Sabbath."

"Perhaps so." ·

I felt the pang that smote on Annie's heart at the implied censure for her weary looks. I felt the pang; but no thrill of pleasure at the compliment. I almost hate Annie's husband. He does n't mean it, Annie says; he don't know how it hurts If he could only be hurt in the same way just enough to appreciate the pain he is so ingenious in thoughtlessly contriving for her! It is not thoughtlessness; he is purposely urging her up to improve her looks, — to perform an impossibility.

"As ye would that others should do unto you," is a good precept; but sometimes there is more worldly wisdom in doing unto others as they do unto you. The love that holds the rod is just as true love as that which smooths the path. Ah truer! It endures the pain of inflicting pain, the severest pain that love can endure for the good of the loved.

It is said to be with woman as with the canine ‘ species : the more the rod is used upon her, the more closely she will cling to him who wields it. There is certainly fear engendered toward a tormentor, where he has the authority to control, and the power to inflict suffering; but if the infliction of torture generates love, unless the chastisement administered be deserved on account of offense committed, why it is so, is among the mysteries of human nature.

Perhaps the individual instances which have gone
to make up the popular proverb, if traced to their
source, might prove surreptitious facts. If the husband held the rod in public, Mrs. Caudle may have
wielded the darning-needle, or the broom-handle
when there was no eye to see, and no tongue to report it. Being really even, there need be no dim-
inution of love.

May be it is the nature of human love to bear the
lash and love on. May be it is in the same human
nature to use the lash and love on. A consciousness
of deserving chastisement is a wonderful stimulant to
endurance, as the consciousness of receiving wrong
is to resentment. But that the sting, from the un-
deserved application of the lash, should excite or
stimulate love, may be reckoned among the mysterious developments of human nature, yet unfathomed;
or rather to domestic mysteries, unseen by common
acquaintances.

That one half the married people remain together
from other motives than the desire to do so, is no
"guess." Sometimes one motive operates to keep
the hymenial knot tied through life, and sometimes
another; but how often is it love after a few years
of felicity have passed over the heads of the happy
pair? Every one has the liberty to answer for him
or herself.

XX.

MRS. NED JONES came in to-day to make a call, and her husband with her.

Ned rudely began to make his comments, as his wife looked at goods and asked prices.

He went on accusing milliners with making enormous profits. Ned keeps a store himself, and ought to know better. People that live in glass houses ought to be careful how they throw stones. I let him finish his tirade against our offending craft, and then I turned upon him, —

"Is it because milliners are worse than other tradespeople that I hear so much about their derelictions ? If I had opened a confectionery store would n't I have been made just as familiar with the sins of confectioners, by my customers, as I now am with those of milliners? Verily I may in the exercise of all charity so judge human duality. The cause of such a state of things is very evident to observers, if not to those interested in berating milliners."

A person wishing to buy an article depreciates the first cost of it in order to lessen the amount of profit to the seller, and get it at a low rate for himself. Ned never supposed, when he was telling me that

12

my goods did n't cost me half I asked for them,
that he was putting his motive for so doing before
me, and also his own habits of trading.   He thought
he was showing me up.   I thought he was showing
himself up.   Who was he showing up?   Evil-minded
people, that are determined to make evil meaning
on all sides, would say, both were shown up.

I said to Ned, in a caustic way, — no doubt I intended to be sharp, and cut him up as much as he
had me ; was that retaliation? very likely; I am
only a poor erring human dual like my fellows, —
" It is very easy to tell what your profits have been.
Look at the fine house you have built up town, and
the handsome furniture in it, and there need be no
questions asked as to your profits !   It is no myth that
you have made profits, and it is no mystery where
you have bestowed them.   If you don't wish to have
such examples followed, you ought not to set them.
Others do as we do, not as we say.   Such is the,
force of example, and the weakness of precept."

" You must remember that our house is the profits of twenty years' business.   Ned has been in business twenty years," said his wife eagerly.

" Well, Mrs. Jones, if I can live as you live, and
have lived for twenty years, I will be satisfied with
my profits."

" Do you notice that lady with Mrs. Jones ? " asked
Gracie ; " we call her the old fashion-plate.   Don't
she look like one ?   It is Mrs. Van Cornet.   She has
been very stylish, and led the fashions here for a

great many years ; but her day is over, and she don't know it. She holds on to her past honors, and makes herself a butt for the younger ladies.

JUNE 26, 18—.

Mrs. Aikin came in with Mrs. Perry to-day, when she came to order her bonnet. After they had "looked" awhile in Mrs. Perry's behalf, she turned to Mrs. Aikin, and asked, —

" What are you going to have ? "

"I went out of town for mine. Styles are so all alike here, I wanted something different."

After she went out, Gracie said to me, " Did you see what airs Mrs. Aikin put on, when she talked about going out of town for her bonnet ? The truth is, they are real poor if her husband is a professional man. It is just as much as they can do to keep up appearances, and all her airs are shams. She is obliged to economize just as closely as possible, and she is ashamed to do it here ; she is afraid all her acquaintances will find it out, and laugh about her ; so she goes out of town to get her things, where she thinks she is n't known. But the expedient is very much of a muchness. They all know it, and laugh to think she is so foolish."

XXI.

You were not at Sabbath-school yesterday morning; were you ill, Gracie?" I asked of her this forenoon.

"No ma'am," she answered with a scarlet face.

I saw that something was wrong, and I asked again,—

"Was your mother or sister ill?"

"No'm." She saw that I was bent on knowing why she was absent, and she went on: "I know you'll think I did wrong; I trimmed a bonnet in the morning."

"Was it a mourning bonnet for a funeral? If so, I should think it no wrong."

"It was n't. It was a bonnet for a neighbor."

"Then why did you do it?"

"Because she came in, and begged me to. She said it was an old bonnet, and not worth carrying to the shop; but she wanted me to do it. —she thought I could make is look as nice as though it came here."

"So she flattered you into breaking the Sabbath, little Gyp?"

"Not entirely; she said, she hated to have me do it Sunday, and she hated to have me stay at home

from Sunday-school, but she could n't go to meeting
without it, and there was some one going to preach
that she wanted to hear very much. She had been
very kind to mother, especially when she was sick
last summer, and so I did it."

Perhaps the good woman got more benefit from
that sermon than Gracie would have acquired at the
Sabbath-school. Perhaps that one job of work did
more to establish ideas of practical religion in Gracie's mind than a row of Sabbath-schools reaching
across the Atlantic could have done. She is an
apt scholar, like most girls in their teens.

"Did she pay you for doing it?" I asked.

" Certainly. She belongs to the church, and she
said she did n't approve of working Sunday."

"Thou, nor thy maid-servant," suggested the
inner. It is astonishing how inclination will modify devotion. In the same ratio will interest modify
principle. The command does not extend to thy
neighbor's maid-servant; therefore, the good woman
might not consider herself responsible for keeping
Gracie at work.

She was a frequenter of the sanctuary, and an observer of the Sabbath; but, given to literal construc-
tions of the teachings she heard. She did n't understand that she had any thing to do with keeping her
neighbors' servants out of mischief, or any responsibility if she helped them into it. Perhaps not.

" Did she pay you as much as it would have cost
her if she had brought it here?"

" Not quite," said Gracie with another blush. " I
know just how mean I was, and I tried to get her to
bring it here. I told her I had no right to use the
knowledge I got here for my own benefit, out of the
shop ; that all I could do in the way of millinery belonged to you ; but she had been so kind to mother
I could n't help obliging her. The bonnet was a
shocking old thing, and well deserves its time, if
long service can buy it. It has served as long as
Jacob did for Rachel, and will probably have the
honor of doubling its time as he did, if it will hold
together."

JUNE 28, 18—.

How can one be expected to be very amiable after
having dissipated all night at a musquito concert?
Such is my case. I am not naturalist enough to
bear their songs for the sake of science; so I made
an onslaught. Not with the care of a taxidermist
seeking to preserve their frames for mounting ; but
I mercilessly crushed the little things to death, without the slightest compunction at destroying so much
musical talent. It was without effect. I could not
disperse them. As fast as I slaughtered, multitudes
of first cousins refilled the orchestra and piped out
requiems over the untimely graves of the fallen.
The unseasonable serenade made a very bad impression upon my nerves.

Right upon this state of mind pounced an out-of-
town customer. She ought to have exercised more
discretion than to have come in contact with my

nervous excitability, after so trying a night; but the selfish thing went on in her own way, without paying the slightest heed to my condition. She commenced: " I have brought you a bonnet to be done over, but I don't want it done like the one you did for Mrs. Powers; I stopped there as I came along, and she showed it to me. It looked dreadfully. It was n't fit to wear ; " and so she went on for about five minutes.

Had those musquitoes undergone transmigration ? had they run violently into this woman's tongue, in order to punish my blood-thirsty disposition ? They were easier to deal with in their original state. I could n't slap this woman between my palms, and crush her out of the way. I might spring my tongue upon her, as she had done hers upon me, and I did.

" Do you take in fault-finding to do for your neighbors? " I asked. " If you do, I would like to ask your rates. We have a great deal on hand that ought to be done ; if you work for reasonable wages I will furnish you a job. You seem to be mistress of your business."

She was taken all aback ; and her husband, who stood at her elbow, began to chuckle. I went on : —

" We don't get time to attend to it, and we don't think much of its efficacy in ordinary cases ; but there are times when, judiciously applied, it has worked wonders. From the way you accomplished yours I thought it might be agreeable employment;

I thought you might not have enough of your own to attend to, by your performing it for your neighbors. There is no harm in asking, I hope ?"

With an almost uproarious laugh, her husband said to her, —

"There, Sarah, you 've got just what you deserved. Now tell her what you want. You know I 'm in a hurry."

With a crest-fallen, humble look, she turned to me, and said, —

"I did n't intend to find fault."

"I have no idea that you formed such a purpose definitely in your mind, and executed it for that end ; but if you look it over you will see that is just what you did. If I don't do work to suit you, your remedy is to take it to some one that will. If I do it, and it don't suit you, I am willing to be told when I fail ; but it is hardly necessary to lecture me in advance, or on other people's account."

"She 's told you the truth, Sarah, and I hope you 'll remember it ; " said her husband, still laughing heartily. "Come, be expeditious."

I don't suppose her husband was any more reasonable than other men, but he was a store-keeper, and understood the merits of the case.

It need not be inferred from this, that, under all circumstances, in sickness and in health, men, as a class, are any more reasonable than women ; but it is usually easier to trade with them, because they know in a very short time if they will take a thing; or if they will leave it, which manner of dealing saves time.

That woman had the root of the matter in her. She turned to me with a pleasant smile, and said, —

" I really did n't intend to find fault. Perhaps you won't be willing to do my bonnet?"

" Certainly; I will do your bonnet, and make it look as well as I can; but I can't make an old bonnet look as well as, or better than, a new one. Sometimes bonnets come from the bleach looking very nicely, and sometimes they are scarcely improved at all. Sometimes when they look badly it is the fault of the straw, and sometimes of the owner. If they are worn a long time, they get so badly sunburnt it is impossible to make them white. I think my bleacher does his best to make them look well."

She selected her trimmings, with her husband's help, and gave the rest of her order very expeditiously.

XXII.

THIS morning I was summoned into the front shop to see a lady on very urgent business. She was in such haste she could n't wait a moment.

I dropped the work that was driving me like dust before the wind, and rushed in hot haste to receive her commands. When I entered, I saw rather a fine looking woman, on the other side of the store, deliberately selecting and cheapening some goods.

I stood fifteen or twenty minutes waiting for her to come and unfold the cause of her marvelous haste, which seemed to evanesce with my appearance.

When she had finished up on the other side, she walked slowly over to where I stood, counting her change as she came. When that preliminary was accomplished, her purse was safely deposited in her pocket. Then she asked, —

" Have you any mourning bonnets?"

"I have some frames covered," I replied, "which can be finished in a short time."

"Would you be kind enough to lend me one? My husband died Saturday," — this was Monday morning, — "and is to be buried to-morrow. I have got to buy one, but I want time to look round, so as to buy to the best advantage; so I thought I'd borrow one for the funeral."

Spirit of economy! Spirit of the departed husband, whose lifeless clay still lay in her home, explain to me, if you can, what kind of humanity is that woman made up of! No doubt the ghostly partner of her former connubial joys could tell with mathematical certainty, if his tongue were only permitted to exercise its former elasticity. It is unnecessary, she explains herself.

If an ice-house had been discharged at me, I would n't have been more coolly prostrated by the blow. I stared at her in my astonishment, and echoed in my wonder, —

" Lend you a bonnet! "

She did n't seem to perceive that she was doing any thing out of the common way. She did n't perceive my surprise, but went on to state inducements for me to confer so unusual a favor upon her widowhood : —

"I intend to buy a bonnet, and shall probably come here; but I want to take time to look round, and see where I can do best."

Explain such a phenomenon, ye who can! It is past my comprehension! Her husband died scarce two days before; and with due, or undue regard to the temporal interests of the little pledges which he had left orphaned upon her hands, she had left his lifeless remains in the kindly care of some neighbors, and gone out shopping.

If she had locked up the lucre for which he had toiled, in caution lest it take its flight and follow him to pave his part of eternity's golden streets, or mount the pearls of its immortal gates, as he had always kept the keys on earth, where would have been the wonder? But that was by no means the case. Her care was, that no more of it than she could not possibly prevent should pass into the hands of contemporary sinners.

Was it the strong mother-love about which so much poetry is made, that sent her out to save a few pennies in her purchases? Was it the stronger love of lucre that burnt at the ends of her itching fingers, and destroyed the tenderness which would have drawn most hearts, in the last, clinging love to perform the last sad office to their dead, while their shopping was intrusted to other hands?

That the love of money may so benumb the sensibilities, that woman is proof.

Right upon the steps of the new-made, worldly-minded widow, came little Mrs. Fluttery. This is the seventh time she has made it in her way to come in, and talk over her bonnet. Six times before this has the exquisite little thing gone through the preliminaries to the advent of a new bonnet. So says Gracie, who has tied knots in a string to keep the tally of her visits.

She comes flying in each time, and repeats her role. Whether it has been written out, and committed to memory, I cannot tell; but it is stereotyped in form, and repeated as punctiliously as the Liturgy in church. If it is an extempore performance, her thoughts always run in the same channel. If Nature furnished her with but one set of ideas, she furnished her with but one form to express them in, and it is after this fashion : —

" I know you are tired to death of me, but I can't help it. I don't know what I want, and you must tell me ; and if you tell me I sha'n't know any better than I did before.

" Blue is the prettiest color in the world for me, but I 've worn it forever and forever, and I want a change. Charley hates green, — I can't have that, and buff is worn by every servant-girl on the streets now. Brown is too old for me, and black makes me think of a pall. White reminds me of a winding-sheet, and sets me shivering. Lavender and purple are beautiful colors, but they don't suit my complexion."

" Plaids," I suggested.

" They remind me of factory girls and ginghams. No! I can't bear plaids!"

" A dark, rich pink is considered pretty now."

" Pink!" she echoed with a gesture of terror. " Pink, and Magenta, and Solferino, and scarlet, — the whole class of reds are an abomination to the rainbow. The very thought of them sets me ablaze! I should look like a full moon set out with a signal of distress. Can't you think of something else?"

" I will take your case into consideration.   If it is possible to invent another pirmordial you shall have the benefit of the color.   But I continue very much of my formerly expressed opinion, that you will be obliged to take some combination, — brown and white with a bit of blue, or drab and blue, or drab and buff, or something of the sort.   I 'll think it over."

And her case went into consideration, — the state in which it has rejoiced so far into the season, and where it seems fated to remain for an indefinite period.

XXIII.

I SPENT the day at Annie Drew's yesterday. George followed us up so closely I thought I never should get a chance to give Annie the advantage of my experience in life. He was very anxious to show me, and receive praise for, all the comforts with which he had surrounded her. He had provided every thing heart could wish, and of course I could n't retain the meed due.

In the midst of it all he made her miserable by continually praising other ladies who were exactly her opposite in looks and manners. It sounded like a reproach to her. Annie is not of a mean, envious disposition, and if it were not implied in the praise of others that she did n't do her part as he does his, she would have rejoiced in it rather than have been pained by it. It was her implied deficiency that humbled her, and made her unhappy, and disheartened her.

After dinner came the inevitable smoke and nap. For once I blessed the invention of cigars !

When he had got well under way, and no interruption threatened, I drew up close to Annie, put my arm around her, took her hand in mine, just as

we used to sit when we were school-girls. I wound
my will around hers with all my might, to bring her
to my purpose. I understood that her tenderness
for George would interfere with my plan; then I
said to her, —

"Now, Annie, you have every desire of your heart
gratified, and one of the best husbands in the world;"
(It is excellent policy, if you wish to bring a person
over to a disagreeable view of a thing, to pave the
way with praise on some other point. Let one see
that you appreciate the good qualities of an object,
and then, if you censure the faults you will be listened to on account of your candor. No one likes
one-sided, uncharitable judgments passed upon themselves, or their friends,) "but I can't help seeing
that you have a heart-ache, and feeling it too. And
I would n't touch it if I did n't think I could help it.
George does not think you inferior to the women he
praises. That is n't what he has in his mind. His
motive is to stimulate you to make the most of yourself, and he don't understand that he is dishearten-
ing you, making you more feeble, and unable to become like what he praises."

She burst into tears.

"I know it makes you feel badly, but tears are no
remedy for the evil. The truth is, and he thinks it,
that you are really superior to the ladies that he
praises. You belong to him, and he wants you to
reflect so much honor upon him, that if you were an
angel he would want you to appear an archangel.

It is wrong, and very thoughtless for him to talk as he does, and I think you can cure him of it if you will."

" If I could only become what he wishes me to be, and admires so much ! "

" Nonsense ! Make him admire you for what you are. Try to be nothing but a good, loving wife and mother, as you are, and stop fretting because you are not something else. You are not perfect. If you were you would be no fit associate for that excellent husband of yours. He has one fault that is evident to all that see him."

She was touched. She could n't bear that I should see a fault in her faultless, and place it before her. Her eyes began to open. I was drawing her to my views. " That fault you can correct if you will."

" How can I correct him ? " she asked. The idea was almost sacrilege. It was destroying her household gods.

" Every time he praises another woman, instead of letting it cut you, like the drawing of a sharp knife, turn it over, and take the blunted edge. Agree with him, but draw no inferences with regard to yourself. Praise her, and her husband too, if she has one. If she has n't, praise some other fine-looking man. Praise every gentleman where there is any possible opportunity, in season and out of season, as he does ladies. Do it gently and quietly, so that it may not seem forced."

13

"I'm afraid it will hurt his feelings," she said slowly, but I saw that the idea took.

"Just as it does yours, perhaps it will; but if it break up his habit of doing the same thing, it will make him appear much better in the eyes of his acquaintance."

That argument had the desired effect. Her face brightened.

"There can be no harm in trying it. I really do my best to please him, and there is no one but can be found fault with if we allow ourselves in the habit of carping."

"Don't forget it, or fear to try your experiment."

At tea I saw my plan begin to work. Two gentlemen of their acquaintance came in for as large a share of her admiration as other ladies did for his. But I noticed it had a different operation upon him from what it had upon her. He seemed a little disposed to resent it, as some wrong done to himself, and undertook some pretty smart strictures upon the parties wherein his wife had discovered so much merit.

Annie was really bright and cheerful, like her old self. If any mischief comes of it I shall tell the whole story, and take the blame. Otherwise he need be no wiser for my plotting.

But it strikes me a little oddly that George should be fretted because Annie praised other gentlemen. How came he to be possessed of such a feminine trait? His mother must have been a woman, and he must have inherited a part of her character.

XXIV.

" CHILDREN and fools tell the truth."

Such was the case of Katie Doane, a Miss of fourteen who had set her heart, or her fancy, on a new bonnet. This special object of the young lady had been thwarted by her elder sister, Miss Agnes Doane. " Sister Aggie" had been in society two years, and was still without an establishment, or the secure prospect of one. Several admirers had been fluttering around; but nothing eligible had as yet been brought to the sticking-point.

" Precisely the thing" has made his appearance, and is to be secured if possible. The how, is the special subject under consideration in the family at the present time.

The eligibility is a son of one of the " first families;" but he is as fastidious in his taste, and as cautious as to caste and qualifications as the young lady herself.

Style and dress are the desideratum with her; but with him there is a desideratum of the desideratum to be considered, — the means to attain the desideratum. She is thoughtless of that consideration, never having had any care of providing further than

the desideratum. She is ignorant that he may consider it for his interest to make himself acquainted
with the state of her prospects for providing herself
with the desideratum. She is too young and unso-
phisticated to suspect that he may pay sly regard to
the affairs of a certain venerable individual who now
has that prospective consideration in charge.

She is judging of him by herself, not always a
safe standard for a lady to judge a gentleman by.
Owing to the different motives that actuate the different sexes in seeking marriage, the different parts
they are to act, or play as the case may be, and the
different circumstances that are to surround them in
that relation, it is wiser to find out what men really
do think, rather than take it for granted that they
think as a woman does. It may safely be taken for
granted that men do not think as women do in the
prospect of marriage. And it may as safely be
taken for granted that both parties have common
sympathies on one point in view of the event. Each
contemplates the probable advantage to accrue
therefrom to his or her individual duality.

According to Aggie's judgment of the ultimatum
required by the son of one of the first families, she
acted. Dress must be obtained in order to obtain
him, or what he could confer upon her. She had
knowledge enough of her mother's nature to understand what manner of temper to exercise in order
to procure the forthcoming of the desideratum.

By arbitrary exactions, she compelled her mother

and younger sister to practice the beautiful virtue of self-abnegation in her favor. Katie did n't at all relish the practice of self-denial required for the benefit of her elder sister, and in the grief, anger, and disappointment of being subjected to such sacrifice, she fulfilled the old proverb of children telling the truth.

In consequence of being connected with that disappointment I became her confidante. A few days ago she told me what kind of a bonnet she was going to have made, and I had reserved the materials for it.

With choking sobs and tears, she told me how she was to be disappointed.

" Is n't it too bad Aggie must have the whole, when I only want such a little part, and I want it so much. I can't tell you half Aggie has, but it is dozens and dozens of dresses and bonnets, and I only want this one. Mother says she must have it, so she can get married, and when she is gone, and she don't have her to dress, I shall have it all. Only think ! two years I 've had to go without any thing, and I don't see as she is any nearer getting married than she was when she first came out. If she keeps on there won't be any thing left for me, and I shall have to get married the best way I can, without any dress."

I pitied the child, and tried to reconcile her to the circumstances she was placed in. I asked her, —

" Don't you think you might be as happy without so much dress as Aggie is with it ? "

" No, indeed ! nobody will have me if I don't dress. They 'll all think father is poor."

The child expressed the genuine grief that wrung her heart. Were her ideas, which were the cause of the trouble, indigenous to the dual, or were they the imported vegetation of education? Is human nature, education, or the child, to bear the blame of her grief? She doubtless is the one that suffers; but if justice was meted out who would suffer for it? and will justice ever be meted out? If it is over meted out, when, and where, and how will it be done?

I tried to start another train of thoughts. I said, " They would all marry you for your money then. How would you like that ? "

" I 'd sooner be married for my money than be an old maid! Old maids are detestable !"

" We are what we make ourselves. Don't you think it possible to be a good and happy old maid? "

" No, indeed!" she exclaimed with spirit; and she went on rapidly to vindicate her opinion. " Aggie cried all night last night because she was n't married. Father came home from Boston, and told her a gentleman on the cars asked after her, and said to him, " I suppose she was married long ago." Father said he was ashamed to tell him she was n't. And father told Aggie he thought he had done his part towards it. He had spent enormous sums for her dress, had taken her round to a great many watering-places, and introduced her to a great many gentlemen. And he said he was sorry she could n't make herself attractive enough to any of them to make them wish to marry her. And Aggie cried, and said father did n't want to support her, did n't love her, did n't want her at home, was ashamed of her; and she cried, and cried. And mother says she and I must do without all we can this summer, so Aggie can go to Newport, and see if she can't make a match, so father won't be ashamed of her. I believe mother is just as much ashamed as father, only she pities Aggie. I 'll get married before they have a chance to be ashamed of me, if they 'll only give me the pretty things to show myself in."

O mother of that poor child! if the bare outline of such a human picture does not startle you from the torpor of your ignorance of the way to direct the spirits which you have introduced to life, neither could you be aroused though one arose from the dead to remonstrate with you!

With such ideas of the marriage relation as those two girls have been educated in, to what end will their whole lives be shaped? They will no doubt be married — married? They will be legally united to some man, and the union will prove one of those uncongenial matches, which end in unfortunate family disagreements; which end in a foretaste of the tortures of the nether world, echoed the inner.

If there is a position in this life where actions rebound upon the spirit to kindle the burning that is never quenched, it is in those unholy homes where the solitary gather themselves in families through the gratification of unholy passions.

The parents who teach children to shape their

course to such ends, dare not face fashion with another practice; but they dare face God's wrath, tribulation, and anguish, — the eternal burning of ceaseless regrets.

The records of trade are inexhaustible. The selection of a few incidents from them may prove as agreeable and useful to readers as a more extended recital. Therefore I close my Diary.

THE END.